Blood Brothers

Also by Gary McCarthy

SODBUSTER
THE MUSTANGERS
THE LAST BUFFALO HUNT
MUSTANG FEVER
THE FIRST SHERIFF
THE DERBY MAN

Blood Brothers

GARY McCARTHY

A DOUBLE D WESTERN
DOUBLEDAY
NEW YORK   LONDON   TORONTO   SYDNEY   AUCKLAND

A DOUBLE D WESTERN

PUBLISHED BY DOUBLEDAY

a division of Bantam Doubleday Dell Publishing Group, Inc.
666 Fifth Avenue, New York, New York 10103

DOUBLE D WESTERN, DOUBLEDAY, and the portrayal of
the letters DD are trademarks of Doubleday, a division of
Bantam Doubleday Dell Publishing Group, Inc.

Library of Congress Cataloguing-in-Publication Data applied for

ISBN 0-385-24570-X

For Bill Peterson,
good friend
and son of a mining man

Blood Brothers

CHAPTER ONE

Ben Pope sat atop the peak of Sun Mountain and decided that he was definitely getting drunk. He tested this suspicion by closing first one eye and then the other, to flip back and forth between double and single vision. To hell with it, he thought, refusing to feel at all guilty. He was sixteen and being drunk was about the only form of recreation on Nevada's Comstock Lode. Actually, being drunk was not as exciting as Ben had expected. You giggled some and you burped, but mostly you just sat and watched the world spin while you tried to keep from falling off. That, and you wondered why your best friend wasn't even tipsy despite the fact that he had been matching you drink for drink.

"What do you find so damned interesting down there?" he asked.

Rick Kilbane glanced sideways at him, then turned back to study the sprawling boomtown below. "Everything in Virginia City interests me."

"Not me," Ben said. "It's dry, hot and ugly."

When Rick did not comment, Ben stretched out full. He laced his fingers behind his head and stared up at the azure, cloudless Nevada sky. It revolved in a languid circle around and around, and he tried to imagine he was floating on a swirling cloud and that he was having fun. It wasn't working, but he was not one to quit trying, and Rick sure wasn't proving to be much in the way of company.

"No sir," he drawled, "I sure don't see what you find so fascinating about Virginia City."

"It's the people," Rick said. "Look at 'em! There are thousands and they're all here for the money. No other reason."

"That's for damn sure."

Rick smiled, knowing how his friend hated this country and yearned for escape. Ben was correct when he said the Comstock was ugly. But ugly or not, Rick thought of her as a washed-out lady with powdery-white skin, tired wrinkles, but also with a heart of pure gold and silver. And the lady, despite the fact that both men and machines probed for her heart, just kept giving and giving. Her generosity seemed to be boundless. A fortune had already been torn from her bosom as both men and machines ruthlessly traced her veins, sucking her dry, riddling her weary corpse like so many ravenous maggots until she often belched poisonous gases. No one had to tell Rick that Comstock mining claims were worth thousands of dollars a surface running foot, that her stocks traded on every world market and just kept soaring until every fifth or sixth man in Virginia City claimed himself to be a paper millionaire.

"They say that the Comstock is financing the Union's side of the Civil War," Rick mused aloud. "And there's little doubt she's made San Francisco the greatest banking center west of the Mississippi."

"What?"

Rick shook his head. "Never mind. It isn't important."

"The whiskey makes me feel awful," Ben complained, sitting up and wiping his pale face.

"You don't look too good. Maybe you'd better not drink any more whiskey. You're too heavy for me to carry off this mountain."

Ben nodded. "It's too bad you didn't graduate with me today."

"Why?" Rick said. "Graduation means nothing to me. I learned how to read and write, same as you. I'm good with figures. Better than Pa, even. And look what he's done for himself. He's getting rich off our Silver Dollar Saloon."

The subject of Ulysses Kilbane had always interested Ben. "How many men do you reckon your pa has shot?"

"Enough. Five, maybe six." Rick took the bottle of whiskey and drank deeply. "Men used to try and cheat him at cards. He's killed enough of them that they don't do that anymore."

Ben said, "A lot of people claim Jessie has killed more than twenty."

"That's a bunch of bull," Rick growled, turning his attention back to the high desert vista.

Rick's dark brown eyes missed nothing on the Comstock. Not the heavy wagon traffic, the Chinamen shuffling in and out of their ceremonial "joss" houses or the Paiutes that were leading thin horses up from the desert to sell scraps of mesquite and firewood to the miners. The Comstock drew fortune seekers from all over the world and had even given new life and hope to the desperate Forty-Niners who had panned the Sierra gold streams until there wasn't a Chinaman's chance of making a living off a placer claim.

How those destitute Argonauts must have stood in shocked silence at the crest of the Sierras to gaze eastward from under pine trees into the blistered Nevada deserts! Already, these barren hills were completely stripped of their pinion and juniper pines, all consumed either in fires or by the mountain itself in its hundreds of miles of tunneling. What remained above ground was nothing but sun-blasted mountains, baked white in summer and snow-white in wintertime. On the Comstock, you either roasted or froze, and no man came to the "Big Bonanza," as their renowned journalist, Dan DeQuille had dubbed this place, for his health. Instead, he came for one reason only, and that was to get rich quick and run to wherever he called home with his pockets full of money.

Despite all this, Rick knew he loved the Comstock. Loved the thump-thump sound of the giant rock crushers and the mighty steam engines that strained night and day to drag men and ore up from the belly of Sun Mountain. And now, as he sat holding the bottle of whiskey, he felt rather omniscient as if he were surveying his own kingdom. High from this favored vantage point, the town below seemed like a child's model, and the men and women who filled the streets and boardwalks assumed the tiniest of proportions. Rick knew that many were flat-out evil, for wealth always attracted cutthroats, thieves and murderers. But the vast majority of those he watched were very decent, hard-working souls, each trying to win a stake in the hard game of life.

Rick smiled. The whiskey had outwardly affected him, but inwardly, it made him feel at peace and very charitable toward his fellow man. There was a stiff breeze blowing hot off the eastern desert and he could smell the muddy Carson River almost eight miles away. It would be cool under the cottonwood trees along the Carson. The water would be inviting and there were always fish to be caught, even if the river was jammed by logging because men had stripped bare nearly the entire eastern slope of the Sierras.

Rick made a note to take one of his father's saloon girls for a swim tomorrow. Maybe the new one named Jenny French. Jenny looked like the kind of girl who would want to have a good time with the boss's son. He took a pack of imported Cuban cigarillos from his shirt pocket and shoved one in his mouth. He used his thumbnail to strike a match and when he inhaled, he blew a smoke ring that lassoed the tall steeple of St. Mary's of the Mountain Church. The irony of roping a Roman church steeple with a ring of Mexican smoke struck him as amusing and he chuckled.

"Maybe I'm getting a little drunk myself," he said, more to himself than to his friend. "So what are you going to do about going underground tomorrow?"

"I don't know." Ben's expression grew very somber. "Pa has been bragging to everyone that I'll become the best miner on the Comstock someday."

"You should have told him how you act when you get closed in by tight places."

"I couldn't," Ben said. "I'm the son of five generations of miners going back to Wales. Welshmen are supposed to be bred to work underground."

Rick didn't believe that. "The only thing that's born to go underground are squirrels and gophers. Men were born to walk the earth, not crawl around inside of it."

"Don't ever try to explain that to a Welshman."

"You should have told him years ago after we explored that cave and you went crazy," Rick argued. "You will probably go crazy all over again down in the mines. You could get yourself as well as a lot of others killed."

"I can handle it," Ben said stubbornly. "It's not being underground that does it—it's being closed in real tight that I can't stand. That won't happen tomorrow. An apprentice starts working in the loading and unloading stations. They're as big as your pa's saloon. I can handle that."

Rick didn't think his best friend completely understood how grave things could be in the Comstock mines. "All right, for argument's sake, let's say that you can. But what happens when you have to go into a tunnel and work because someone gets sick or hurt?"

Ben snatched the bottle up and drank deeply. He coughed, sleeved his lips and said in a voice made gravelly by the liquor, "I'll just face that if it comes."

"I could still ask my pa to give you a job as a swamper. You could move up; tend bar in a few years. I could teach you some poker and you'd make a house dealer."

"Thanks, but we've been over this before. My folks would kill me if I worked in a saloon. Besides, even you told me my fingers are too thick for handling cards. Remember?"

"Yeah." Rick studied Ben's hands. Hands that had a grip like an iron trap and that had yanked him playfully off his feet more than once. "Are you pretty damn drunk?"

"I thought I was, but I'm feeling better for the moment. I just wish that we could run off someplace and not come back."

"Not me," Rick said. "This is where I plan to make my stake."

Ben tried to focus on his own four feet. "If I could leave, I'd find a nice place in California and take up farming."

"I'd hate farming."

"It's good work!" Ben said earnestly. "A man takes comfort watching things grow. You've seen my vegetable garden. I've got the touch."

"Maybe, but I'll take a lot more comfort in watching money grow than a few radishes and tomatoes."

Rick stood and hiked a few yards west over the crest of the mountaintop where he could enjoy an entirely new panorama. To the north was Reno, to the south, far, far to the south, was a place called Death Valley. But the view westward was the one that held his eye like the painted canvas of some great master. Hands resting on his narrow hips, cigarillo hanging forgotten from the corner of his mouth, he gazed upon the magnificence of the snow-capped Sierra Nevadas and up closer the green swath of the Carson and Washoe Valleys. Rick could almost taste the pines, and the wind that blew off the highest peaks was cool on his face.

He went back to squat on his heels and study Ben, whose color was not too good. "You gonna get sick on me?"

"Probably."

"Then go ahead and do it, and you'll feel better. Just don't fall asleep on me up here," Rick said. "You're too damned heavy to carry down this mountain."

"Not a chance. I can't stop thinking about tomorrow."

"Just tell your pa you won't go down there."

"I can't do that," Ben said. "What if you told your father you had decided not to have anything to do with his saloon. That you wanted to be . . . oh, say a blacksmith."

"Don't be ridiculous."

"There's nothing ridiculous about it! The point is, you'd disappoint the hell out of him. In fact, I don't think you'd do it any more than I can."

"I would if it meant saving my sanity," Rick said. "Has your pa even told you how deep he's working?"

Ben's voice dropped to a whisper. "He's working at the twelve-hundred-foot level."

Rick's mouth crimped down and he looked away. He could see the huge tin building which housed the machinery and hoisting works of the Lucky Eagle Mine where Ben would start work early tomorrow morning. "At twelve hundred feet, the temperature will be nearly 120 degrees. The air will be bad and you'll swear you were dropped into the bowels of hell."

"Thanks," Ben said. "Any more encouraging news?"

"No, I guess not."

An uncomfortable silence stretched between them until Ben said, "I was thinking of Mandy Nye just now."

Ben had been in love with Mandy for the last two years, but nothing much had come of it because of his shyness. Once, Rick had even considered sparking Mandy himself, but he'd rejected the idea because Mandy was the sheriff's daughter.

"And I was thinking," Ben continued, "if things go okay tomorrow, I might just start courting her."

"Oh really, that'll be the day," Rick said.

"Now what is that supposed to mean?"

"Just that I don't see why you should hurry into anything. I mean, you've only known the poor girl what, three, maybe four years."

"I can talk to her," Ben said defensively. "We talk every time we see each other."

Rick lit another cigarillo. Ben and Mandy were both virgins. As innocent as babes. They deserved each other.

"You know," Ben said, "I sure like Mandy and if I could just earn a miner's wages, I'd buy her an engagement ring."

"Is that why you're really going down there?"

"Partly," Ben confessed. "But I've got to do it for myself, too. And for Pa. Besides, I can't get married without a profession that pays an honest wage and the miner's union just got another raise. I want to marry her, Rick."

"It'll wait a few years. We're only sixteen. A fella should sow some wild oats and have a little fun in life before he puts his shoulders to the wheel."

"You been sowin' your oats since you were thirteen," Ben said, shaking his head. "But someday, you'll get serious about a girl like her."

Rick finished his cigarillo and ground it under his heel. He hadn't realized how serious his friend was about Mandy Nye and it worried him. Ben wasn't near ready for marriage—not by a long shot.

"Listen," Rick said. "In case you haven't figured this out, Sheriff Nye would never let his only daughter marry a miner."

"You don't know that for sure!"

"Oh yes I do. I can tell you for certain that our sheriff doesn't like miners any better than he likes card dealers and saloon owners. He and my pa are going to kill one another someday."

"The sheriff is good, but he's no match in a gunfight with your pa," Ben said. "But never mind that. We're talking about me and Mandy, and I've made up my mind that if I can hold a miner's job, I'll ask her to marry me and if she says yes, then it won't matter what the sheriff says. We'll just go ahead and tie the knot anyway."

"I figured that's what you'd say."

"Well, then," Ben said, still a little ruffled, "why'd you go and tell me the sheriff wouldn't let her marry a miner?"

" 'Cause it's the truth," Rick said. "I heard him say it myself."

Ben swayed to his feet. He stood six-foot-one-inch and his shoulders were sloped with muscle like those of an ox. He had pale brown hair, a heavy brow and jaw, and a wide, generous mouth that generally bore one stage or another of a smile. Everyone who met Ben liked him at first glance. In Rick's opinion, if he had any faults at all, it was that he was too trusting and naive.

They were almost the same height, but that was all they had in common besides a mutual respect and childhood friendship. Ben was easygoing, Rick knew he was often too intense. Ben was built for power, Rick for speed and quickness. When they wrestled, Ben's strength always prevailed, but when they boxed, slapping and moving and having fun, Rick knew that he had the advantage of superior handspeed and reflexes.

Like his father, Rick was gifted with lightning-like reactions. It was in his blood because Ulysses often bragged he'd once had the fastest hands in all of Texas. And he still used this gift to advantage at the card table. Over the last five years, Ulysses Kilbane had parlayed his timing and touch along with an abundance of nerve into more money than any three Comstock miners might earn in their lifetimes.

Ulysses had gone through two wives in five years, one being Rick's mother, and then he spent the last eleven years raising hell. His pleasure was wild women and hard whiskey and even he admitted it was a miracle that he'd saved enough to buy their thriving Silver Dollar Saloon.

"You ready to go down?" Rick asked.

Ben finished the whiskey and hurled the empty bottle end over end to disappear in the thick sagebrush. "Let's go."

"Okay. But if you trip and bust your head, then I'll have to marry Mandy myself."

"The hell you will," Ben growled, starting down the steep, narrow footpath. He turned and said, "You'll keep chasing those saloon girls and all you'll get for your trouble is grief."

"I've got my eye on a new girl at the Silver Dollar whose name is Jenny French. She's sure a looker."

"I'll bet she don't hold a candle to Mandy."

"She's just different is all. Jenny definitely isn't the marrying kind, but then, neither am I."

"Don't you even want kids?"

"Nope."

"You got a stack of poker chips where your heart ought to be."

"Maybe," Rick said, trying to mask his growing irritation. "I'll have a hundred different women and a bank full of cash by the time I'm thirty and you'll have a stack of bills and a cabin full of kids. Then we can compare notes and see who had it figured out best."

Ben shook his head. "I guess we are altogether different. Mandy and a California farm to feed our kids on is my dream."

"To each his own," Rick said. "Let's get back down this mountain before it gets dark."

Ben started down but he took no more than a few steps when he lost his footing and pitched headlong down the trail, sledding on the loose gravel. He pulled out two big clumps of brush before he finally managed to stop and then an avalanche of loose rock nearly buried him alive. When Ben finally staggered to his feet, coughing and choking, his shirt ripped at both the knees and elbows, Rick couldn't help himself and began to laugh.

"Go ahead and laugh your head off if you think it's so damned funny. But if you were down here and if I wasn't a little drunk, I'd grab you by the throat and drag you all the way down to 'C' Street!"

Rick shook his head. He and Ben had known each other for a lot of years and been fast friends since the day they'd gotten in a fight outside of Virginia City's one-room schoolhouse on their very first recess. Ben had gotten the better of the scrape, but Rick had fought so hard that he'd earned everyone's respect—especially the oversized son of a Welsh miner. And despite their differing backgrounds and philosophies, they'd found each other to be trustworthy and ready to help in times of trouble. For six years, they'd been almost inseparable until this past fall when Rick had quit school on his sixteenth birthday and gone to work in his father's saloon full-time.

They were blood brothers, too. And maybe it had been a childish ritual to scrape their wrists with a shard of broken glass and then bind their wounds together and pledge a lasting friendship. But someone said that the Indians did that and it sounded so impressive they'd gone ahead and mixed their blood too. It had been special and the almost invisible scars that the ritual had left on their wrists were a reminder and a source of great pride to them both. They *were* blood brothers and nothing in the world would ever change that, nothing short of death.

It was sundown when they reached "C" Street and stood outside Ulysses Kilbane's rough and notorious Silver Dollar Saloon.

"Thanks for giving me your pa's shirt and the pants," Ben said. "They're both a hell of a lot nicer than anything I ever owned."

"He'll never miss them, he's got so many," Rick said. "Are you sure you don't want a job?"

"I'd be disowned by my family if they found out I was working in a saloon owned by a man who also runs a whorehouse."

Rick was stung. "I guess your pa thinks there is something noble about being poor."

"And I guess there's no sense in us talking about it any longer. I'm going to go down in that mine tomorrow and I'm going to be fine."

"Okay, do that." Rick expelled a deep breath. "But if you go stark raving mad, don't say I didn't warn you."

"I'll be all right," Ben said too quickly. The whiskey had already worn off and made him realize that he'd been pretty insulting. It left his stomach tasting sour and a pounding ache right behind his eyes. "Look, I didn't mean anything about that Jenny girl or your father. I guess drinking whiskey made me mean."

"It does that to some men," Rick said. "See you tomorrow after work?"

"Yeah. It'll be okay down in the mines tomorrow. I promise."

Rick didn't believe that for a moment, but he'd said his peace. "Good, see you then."

Ben turned and walked away. Ulysses' shirt and the pants fit him perfectly and except for his old worn-out work shoes, he almost looked like a successful young merchant.

Rick watched his friend until he disappeared in the crowd

and then he entered his father's saloon. It was packed with rough miners; the piano player was pounding out "Sweet Betsy from Pike" and the roulette wheels were spinning.

Several men greeted Rick warmly, for he was well liked and respected as a first-rate poker and faro player. Slapping shoulders, addressing men by their first names and making his way to the bar to order a beer, Rick felt very much at home and he joined in the singing. He even managed to forget about Ben and what his friend would face early tomorrow morning, twelve hundred feet closer to hell.

CHAPTER TWO

Before daybreak the next morning, Ben's skull felt as if it had been cracked so badly that half his brains had leaked out during the night. He could not think straight and his stomach churned with surly rebellion. But now, as he and his father walked quickly through the early predawn to begin work at the Lucky Eagle Mine, his first hangover paled in comparison to the challenge he must face.

Ben's desperation grew like a wildfire until it threatened to consume him with dread as more and more miners fell in with them. They all carried small metal lunch boxes and wore the same kind of working clothes. Heavy blue flannel pants, a gray or blue woolen shirt, a pair of heavy brogans and a felt hat with a very small brim. Ben's outfit was stiff with newness, but he took no pride in it. The brogans seemed heavy and too large. They squeaked and he knew with certainty that they'd give him blisters before his first twelve-hour shift was over—if he somehow lasted.

No one talked. A few coughed from deep in their lungs and spat phlegm and the rest looked tired and dispirited. Many had already drank or lost today's wages and quite a few had even borrowed money at 20 percent interest against their next week's earnings. A few of the wiser ones had managed to save a couple of dollars, but prices on the Comstock were so outrageous a working miner couldn't seem to get ahead, no matter how many raises the union won for him.

Of all the men, only George Pope seemed to be in an unusually good mood. And why shouldn't he be? He had waited a long time for Ben to join him in the mines. With both of them earning good wages, maybe the family could finally save money and hope for a better life.

"Yes sir!" George bragged loud enough for anyone within fifty yards to hear. "Today the Pope family begins to live good again. I've been supporting Ben for sixteen years and he is finally ready to repay the debt. Ain't that right, Son?"

"Yes sir," Ben said in a wooden voice, thinking that now he at last understood how a man would feel on his last walk to the gallows.

George was too delighted to notice his son's near paralyzing anxiety. "Mark my words, Ben here will be our boss within a few years. He comes from Welsh mining stock and I damn sure taught him the meaning of hard work. Now, he's going to get paid for it."

Ben watched the pale light of first dawn seep across the round, rocky hills to the east and fire them with color. Up ahead, he could see the dark outline of the huge tin building that housed the Lucky Eagle hoisting works. Being one of the largest operations on the Comstock, the building covered almost two solid acres and there were no less than six smokestacks, every one of them trailing off a plume of white steam. Ben thought he could feel the earth shivering as the Comstock excavation proceeded around the clock with feverish intensity.

They arrived at the mine property gates where two powerful and heavily armed guards passed them inside without comment. Soon, the graveyard shift would be brought up and the guards would search every departing miner for contraband ore.

"Mornin'," George said to the guards. "Gonna be hot today."

The shotgun-wielding men said nothing and the dispirited dayshift shuffled past.

When they entered the immense tin building that housed the mining works, Ben felt the hardwood floors tremble as three monstrous steam engines clanked, belched and hissed hot clouds of white steam. Giant boilers sweated as men scurried about watching gauges and using long wrenches to constantly keep the pressure and fittings properly adjusted. Outside, it had still been cool, but inside the tin building, the temperature was already nearing one hundred degrees.

Conversation was impossible because of the din, and for that at least, Ben was grateful. He had never been inside a mining works and it was far more busy and complicated-looking than he would ever have imagined. The mighty engines seemed to rule their scurrying, sweating human tenders and make them look insignificant.

George took him by the arm. There was still a few minutes until the graveyard shift was brought up and he wanted to show his son around. Dodging grim-faced workmen, Ben was led past the blacksmith shop with its glowing-red forges where workmen hammered out steel machine parts, sharpened picks and drills, and rushed to forge metal braces and brackets used both above and beneath the ground. Ben saw what was obviously the carpenter's shop where timbers felled on the eastern Sierra slopes eventually found their way into the whirling blades of huge circular saws. The saws screamed with mad delight each time a timber was ripped and sawdust rooster-tailed fifteen feet into the air. As soon as a board was cut, it was stacked to be used as part of the interlocking square sets which somehow managed to support the incredible stresses they would endure.

George pulled Ben close before shouting in his ear, "I'm earnin' five dollars a month more than these guys who work aboveground. And they have the nerve to call themselves miners!"

George made a face that left little doubt that he held these jobs in low esteem despite the fact that big-time Comstock mining was so mechanized and complex that it took almost as many men working the heavy aboveground equipment as it did working underground. To a Welshman, you had to work deep underground before you earned the right to be called a hard-rock miner.

Ben saw other youths, quite a number of them even younger than himself, working as oilers and assistants. At least a half dozen of them were scurrying around in the machine shop where another steam engine powered lathes, planers, grinders and other machines. Every one of them smoked, leaked oil, banged and clanked in a jarring, discordant protest. The heat, coupled with his uneasy stomach and throbbing head, made Ben feel dizzy and weak. He wanted fresh air and silence. He desperately wanted to bolt outside and never look back. Ben knew that the worst by far was yet to come.

A shrill steam whistle pierced the ear-splitting cacophony with blasts so powerful that they easily drowned out the machines and even the ripping saw blades. It was to signal the graveyard shift's emergence from the depths below and it caused George to grab his son by the arm and pull him around a boiler and come face to face with the dreaded main shaft. Ben's heart filled his mouth and he took an involuntary back-step to watch a huge column of steam flow from the earth to the ceiling where it vaporized and dripped on everyone below.

"There she is!" George shouted as the other men came and took their places in the loading area. "The main shaft!"

Ben watched the rising steam with morbid fascination. The rectangular hole in the wooden floor was about five feet wide and twenty feet in length. This opening was divided into four smaller openings and down each ran a thick belt of woven wire cable. Two of the cables were still, but the other pair were shrieking like witches in hell as they were spun up and around enormous hoisting reels. Ben swallowed drily, wanting to run, but discovered his feet stuck to the floor as if they were nailed.

Two cages filled with sweat-drenched miners bobbed into view. There were about eight miners on each cage and they were caked with a combination of sweat and rock dust from deep down below. Only the whites of their eyes looked clean as they blinked like gophers and then staggered off the cages.

Before they had scarcely unloaded, Ben was shoved along with the others on his shift, and when he stepped on the cage, he felt it bounce lightly up and down. Terror flooded through his body and made him sweat from every pore. He glanced sideways at his father and before he could form a protest, a single iron pipe was locked into place forming a rail around them. The moment it locked, the hoisting operator threw a brake handle and the cage plummeted toward the center of the hot earth.

A yell filled his mouth, but the high-pitched whine of spinning cable drowned out his voice. All was heat and darkness, and he gripped the pipe rail and closed his eyes. The sensation of falling was the most horrible thing he had ever endured and it seemed endless. Ben could not breathe. Wild with panic, he opened his eyes as stations flew upward, flickering as fireflies in the night. Each station was one hundred feet below the next and they passed so quickly that Ben had nothing more than blurry impressions of men and machinery. The heat intensified a degree a second, so that when the cage finally began to slow its descent, it was hellishly hot.

Ben's legs felt as if they were going to buckle, but somehow, when the cage did stop, he was able to move onto solid ground. For the first time, he saw the huge square-set timbering that supported a rock ceiling at least forty feet above a solid wood floor. Ben took a deep breath, tasted the steamy, hot air and was surprised to discover that he had not lost his mind.

"Well, Ben, what do you think?" his father asked with a grin. "These stations have all the comforts of home, eh?"

Ben dipped his chin as the sight filled him with wonder. Immense coal-oil lamps fixed in stout brackets illuminated the entire station as brightly as the noonday sun. The station was neat and very functional. There were three sets of tracks leading in and out of the tunnels and several ore carts ready to be loaded onto a cage and hoisted to the surface.

"Follow me over here and hang your coat on an empty nail," George said, pulling his own coat off.

Ben did as he was told. He could not get over the size of the station and how hospitable it seemed. There were even a few tables and benches for the miners to use when they ate or rested.

"Not bad, huh?" George said, studying his son very closely.

"No, not bad at all."

"If it wasn't for the damn heat and steam, a man could live down here year-round in a lot more comfort than he does above ground. Maybe not this deep, but at five hundred feet, it's like the tropics."

Still dry-mouthed, Ben could only nod his head.

"Down here where it's so hot, it feels real good to come out of the snow in the winter and warm up. But going back up on top at the end of your shift, you being all sweaty and such, it's easy to catch pneumonia. You remember to always cool down slow in the winter before jumping out in the snow or a cold wind."

"I will."

"You work hard, Son," George said as he pulled on a pair of heavy leather work gloves from a work bin. "I've been bragging on you and I know you won't let me down."

"No sir."

"Good. You come from mining stock and you'll take to this like a duck to water. You just work hard and keep your mind on your business and make me proud. Your job will be to keep the supplies stocked and get anything the men working in the stopes and tunnels might need."

Ben listened carefully as his father showed him the neatly arranged boxes holding candles, coils of fuse, drills, hammers, picks, shovels and various repair parts for the ore carts.

"Over here is the ice barrel and each man at this level is allotted a hundred pounds a shift. When they come in from the drifts, you hand them these dippers and let them take what they need. Some will want ice water and there are plenty of cups in that cabinet over there."

"That sounds easy enough," Ben said, feeling a great sense

of relief coursing through his veins. He was going to be all right here! He was going to do just fine!

"You'll have plenty of free time but no rest periods like the working miners," George said.

"I don't mind." He wanted to dance and click his heels, so great was his relief.

"Good. You'll also have to wash cups and keep the station tidy. That means sweeping and such."

George sounded apologetic when he added, "But in a month, two at the most, you'll be replaced by another boy and then you'll be working beside me, doin' a man's work and earnin' a full man's wages of five dollars a day. I tried to get you in with me first thing, but they wouldn't hear of it."

"It's all right," Ben said. "It's only fair I start out at the bottom like this and prove myself."

"I knew you'd say that." George gave him a rough pat on the shoulder and then headed on down the tunnel.

As soon as the miners had disappeared, the regular station attendant came over and extended his grimy hand. "My name is Johnny Sears. Good to meet you."

Johnny Sears was short but powerfully built. He had a square jaw and a nice smile. Ben figured they would become good friends, even though Johnny was a good ten years his senior.

Sears was all business. "You're my replacement. I'm supposed to make sure you know what to order and how to use the bell signal, then I'm being promoted to real mining. This job pays four dollars a day. Mining pays five. A dollar a day makes a big difference to a family man."

"Sure it does." Ben grinned so hard his face ached and Sears looked at him a little strangely.

"You all right?"

"I'm just fine," Ben said, noting how his hangover had vanished completely. Never mind that after a month he'd also be promoted to work beside his father in the close, dangerous drifts and stopes. He could worry about that when the time came. In the meantime, he would be earning a man's wages. Soon, very soon, he would buy Mandy an engagement ring if she'd agree to marry him. And tonight, he could hardly wait to tell Rick about how everything had started off so well. Up on the top of Sun Mountain, Rick had been worried about him. Well, at least for the next month, there was nothing to worry about at all. It now seemed very possible to Ben that he'd finally grown out of his fear of tight places. Rick would be happy for him tonight.

It was ten o'clock the next morning when Rick found Jenny French sitting all alone at one of the tables. Rick moved over to the table, smiled and said, "Mind if I join you?"

Jenny glanced up at him, a refusal already formed until she saw who it was. "Why sure. It's your saloon, ain't it?"

Rick took a chair and found he could not take his eyes off Jenny. No matter how young, most women in her profession looked wrung out in the mornings. Jenny was the rare exception. Her black hair was brushed to a shine and there was no puffiness under her eyes. In fact, she looked as if she'd had a glass of warm milk and then slept the whole night long, instead of entertaining his father's most successful customers.

"Coffee?"

"Sure."

Rick called for two cups from the bartender as he remembered that Jenny had told him that she was from New Orleans. More likely, she was from California's famed Barbary Coast and had arrived on the Comstock Lode here hoping to cash in on the wealth like everyone else. Jenny was probably not even twenty years old, but she gave Rick the impression of somehow being very wise. She had eyes as blue as the waters of nearby Lake Tahoe and every bit as cool and inviting. Her skin was so flawless that she wore no makeup whatsoever, which was almost unheard of among saloon girls. She had full, sensuous lips and perfect white teeth, and when Rick looked at her mouth, he wondered why she hadn't married some professional banker or lawyer. She was so desirable that she could have had almost any man she chose.

When the coffee arrived, Jenny sipped hers and said, "So, how does it feel to be the boss's son?"

The directness of the question caught him off balance and he recovered enough to say, "I've never given it a moment's thought."

Jenny almost laughed. "Of course you have. Anyone would feel good knowing they were going to inherit all this." Jenny waved her hand at the chandeliers, the thousand-dollar back-bar mirror, the pictures and the dark, glossy-topped bar, hand-carved in Germany, that ran along one entire side of the room. "Anyone at all."

"The reason I don't think about it, Miss French, is that the Comstock Lode could fail any day. No strike is inexhaustible. Or we might have another big fire and this saloon along with the whole damn city might burn to the ground. Lots of disastrous things could happen, and overnight, I'd be poorer than a Nevada Paiute.

Jenny smiled and made it obvious that she did not take him

too seriously. "Highly unlikely. You are going to be a very, very successful man. Even more successful than your father."

"Why do you think that?"

"Because, you're already much smoother," she told him without hesitation. "Your father reacts to things—but you think about them first."

"Go on," Rick said, aware that she was playing him like a fish and that he did not particularly mind.

She shrugged her pretty shoulders and sipped more of her coffee. "There's not much more to say. I have the impression that you are always thinking. Always calculating the angles so that you can figure out everyone and beat them at their own game."

Rick leaned forward, his eyes boring into hers. "And what is *your* game, Miss French?"

She laughed gaily. "Money, of course! The same as yours. I want fame and wealth and the freedom to do exactly what I want, when I want."

Jenny batted her eyelashes. "Now then, does my honesty shock you?"

"No."

Rick reached for a cigarillo and Jenny had a match in her hand before the cigarillo touched his lips. She lit his smoke and said, "Rick Kilbane, you are a man who will do whatever you have to do to be successful. And I admire that very much."

"Are you always this . . . direct?"

"Yes," she admitted. "Do you believe in astrology, numerology or crystal balls?"

"Of course not."

"Well, I do," she said brightly. "I also believe in palmistry. May I see your palm."

He reacted by pulling his hand back. When she giggled, he felt foolish and stuck it out again. "Go ahead. Amuse yourself."

She took his hand and turned it over so she could study his palm. "Oh!"

He waited, and when she didn't say anything more, he grew impatient. "Oh, what?"

"Oh, you have a very exciting life in store."

"Will I live long and be rich?"

"I already said you'd be successful." Her brows knitted with concentration as she studied his hand. "But I see something here that means you will come to a very grave crossroad early in life."

He leaned over his own hand and studied it intently. "Where?"

"Here." She had long, red-painted fingernails that matched her bright lipstick and she used a fingernail to trace a deep crease across his palm. "This is your lifeline. Here is where the crossroad comes."

Rick couldn't stop looking at her blue eyes and full lips. The palm of his hand that she held glistened damply. "Let me see *your* hand."

She gave him her own hand, and when they laid them side to side, she exclaimed, "Look! See how you have one more deep line branching off from your lifeline than I do? That is the big question mark. I think it will come in four or five years."

Rick found himself a little exasperated when she pushed his hand away. "Is that all you can tell me?"

"No," she said, her voice quiet. "But it is all I *will* tell you right now."

Rick frowned, knowing he could not order her to tell him more. "I want you to come along with me on a buggy ride down to the Carson River."

She pulled her hand away and looked at him with amusement. "Why?"

"So we can have a picnic and go for a swim."

She liked the idea. "If you can swing it with your father, then sure I'll go. It will be fun."

"I'll clear it with Ulysses," he promised. "I'll go wake him up right now."

"You better not. He had quite a load of whiskey in him last night and he's bound to be a little salty this morning."

"He'll live," Rick said, climbing to his feet and heading upstairs where his father and he lived along with a few of the girls. "Get your picnic dress on and bring something to wear in the river. It'll be hot today."

Rick did not even bother to knock at his father's door but slid the key into the lock and marched inside. He had not expected Ulysses to be sleeping alone and he wasn't. There were two women with him in the bed, a couple of floozies who had signed on the payroll about a month ago. All three were snoring.

Rick shook his head. He studied the cigar butts, the over-flowing ashtrays and the two empty fifths of whiskey. Ulysses was getting too old for this; the man could not keep on burning his wick at both ends.

Asleep, Ulysses lost that fierce expression that intimidated all but the most confident men. His wild gray shock of hair ran into an even wilder gray beard. He had the bushiest salt-

and-pepper eyebrows of any man on the Comstock and he was big. Not especially tall, but just plain big allover like Ben Pope. The only thing that wasn't rough about Ulysses was his hands. They'd never held a pick or shovel, or a rope or a plow. Only women, whiskey and cards.

"Pa," he said, grabbing Ulysses' toe and shaking it hard. "Wake up a minute."

Ulysses was not an easy man to wake up after spending most of the night drinking and fornicating. Rick opened the drawn curtains and flooded the room with sunlight. His father groaned in protest, and when Rick finally did get him to open one eye, he growled, "Whatcha mean bargin' in here at day-break! Do you want me to kick the hell out of you!"

"No sir," Rick said, admiring how the floozies could sleep through such loud talk and intense daylight. "And I'm sorry to wake you, but I want to take Jenny French for a buggy ride to the river."

Ulysses wasn't one bit pleased as he knuckled his bloodshot eyes. "There goes at least fifty dollars."

"Jenny hasn't had a day off in two weeks." That much was true. "She looks worn out." The second part was definitely a lie.

Ulysses scratched his hairy chest. His mouth worked silently as he weighed the request. He employed nine women. Jenny was by far his greatest prize. "You better take good care of her. Pack a gun if you take her out of town."

"I already planned to," Rick said. "A woman like Jenny can put foolish ideas into a man's head."

"All right then, take her and keep her until tomorrow—if she wants you."

"She'll want me," he said. "She says I'm a lot like you, only smoother."

"Ha! Of course you're smoother! You got no damn scars or wrinkles yet. Babes and brats are always smooth. Now get the hell outa here so I can go back to sleep. It's still morning!"

Rick moved quickly because what Ulysses Kilbane gave, he could—and often did—take away.

CHAPTER THREE

Rick hired a buggy and drove it around in front of the saloon where Jenny was waiting. "Hop in!"

Jenny stepped off the boardwalk, a smile of anticipation on her pretty face until a big man with a scar across his cheek grabbed her arm and said, "Missy, why don't you tell the kid to drive off by himself and we can go upstairs and have some grown-up fun."

"Get your hands off her," Rick said, wrapping the lines around the brake and stepping down.

The man was mean-looking and he had been drinking. Rick had never seen him before, but everything about him telegraphed danger. He was about to take Jenny's arm and step between them when another man standing on the boardwalk said, "Kid, you best do as Muley says or he'll stomp the hell outa you."

Jenny proved to be a woman of action. She reared back and slapped the man in the face—hard. He jerked her off her feet and pulled her to his chest. "I want you to come with me and Joe Bob upstairs, honey. Don't worry, we got money, plenty of money."

Rick jumped forward. His left hand grabbed a fistful of the man's shirt and pulled him around. His right hand was a blur as it traveled a distance of no more than a foot. His fist smashed Muley alongside of his jaw and wobbled him, but the man recovered and lashed out with his boot. It caught Rick just above his knee and he groaned with pain. When Muley grabbed him by the throat, Rick knew he was in serious trouble. The man's thumbs bit into his flesh and he was powerful. Rick tried grabbing Muley's wrists and breaking his hold, but Muley bent him over the side of the buggy.

"Let go of him, damn you!" Jenny cried, grabbing the buggy whip. "I said let go!"

Jenny lashed Muley across the back and he squealed with pain, "Damn you, stop it!"

In answer, Jenny lashed him again. The whip came down so hard that you could hear it whistle through the air, and when it struck Muley, it left a damp line of blood to soak into the back of his shirt.

Muley let go of Rick's throat. He swung around and grabbed the whip, yanking Jenny completely off her feet. "I'll teach you a . . ."

"Hold it!" Rick shouted, drawing his gun. "Drop the whip and turn around slow or I'll shoot you where you stand."

Muley dropped the whip and his face was a mask of hatred. "Put it away, kid. Put the gun away or I'll feed it to you."

In reply, Rick thumbed back the hammer.

Muley stared at the unwavering barrel, then looked to his brother. "Joe Bob, what are we gonna do about this!"

Joe Bob had already moved and his hand was now resting on the butt of his gun. When he spoke, his manner was so conversational it was almost as if he were talking about the weather. "Well now," he said, "we have a hard decision to make, don't we? I think the kid is all bluff. He's got himself a fancy buggy and he's wearing that nice new shirt. Looks like a sissy to me. I say we call his bluff. He sure don't look stupid enough to face the both of us, are you, kid?"

"Don't bet your lives on it," Rick said, feeling his heart pound faster.

Muley cocked his head to one side. He grinned and showed a row of corn-yellow teeth. "You better put that gun away," he said. "You're startin' to rile the both of us and when . . ."

"Look out!" Jenny cried as Joe Bob went for his gun. Rick saw him out of the corner of his eye, swung his own Colt around and fired twice. The shots were spaced so tightly together that they almost sounded like one. Joe Bob took two mincing little backsteps and slammed up against the Silver Dollar. His face bore a look of complete astonishment as he began to slide down the front of the saloon until he was resting in a sitting position.

Muley stared at his brother for a moment and then he went for his own gun. It was a stupid, drunken and a fatal mistake. Rick twisted and shot him once through the chest. Muley sagged to his knees and tried to finish his draw. Rick didn't wait to see if he was man enough to get his weapon up and then pull the trigger. He shot him once more in the forehead and Muley's eyes rolled up and he crashed forward into the street.

Jenny French was the first to react. She stepped forward, raised her dress and climbed into the buggy. "I'm ready if you are," she said in a voice that trembled only a little.

Without a word, Rick holstered his sixgun and climbed in beside her before he unwrapped the lines.

From up above, the whole town heard Ulysses Kilbane shout, "Nice shootin', son! Next time a man does that to you, shoot him through the guts so he'll die slow!"

Rick glanced up at his father, nodded slightly and then drove through a gathering crowd and headed for a good day on the Carson River. It wasn't until they reached Silver City that Jenny said, "You did that well. Like you've killed men before."

Rick did not say anything.

She leaned very close. "Have you killed men before?"

He tried to speak, but his voice came out sounding tortured because it had almost been crushed. "No."

Jenny draped an arm across his shoulders. She reached up and stroked his bruised throat with her fingertips. "I thought he was going to break your neck. I was so scared he was going to kill you. I didn't think to bring my derringer and I felt helpless. But you were magnificent!"

Rick smiled. "Keep rubbing," he said.

Jenny laid her head against his shoulder and her fingers stroked the bruised place until it felt better. "You know what? I think you are a hero. And I think you and I are going to become lovers."

"It's what I had in mind," he said, his mind replaying how he had killed two men in less than two seconds. Ulysses had insisted he practice with a gun from the moment he was strong enough to raise and aim one. First just for marksmanship, then for speed until he was good, very good. But Rick had always wondered, when the moment had come, if . . . well, he would wonder no more. The training by his father, the talks about gunfighting, they had paid off with his life.

"Do you know a place where we can swim without bathing suits?" she asked.

"That's where I was heading all along."

Jenny kissed him on the cheek and her voice was gay and

girlish. "I've known a lot of men—too many too soon—but you're my only hero! You ever have a hero of your very own?"

"Yeah."

"Who?"

"My father," he said. "Ulysses is my hero."

Jenny leaned out and stared at him. "Are you serious?"

"I am."

She sighed. "Well, he *is* your father."

It was after dark before they returned to Virginia City and Rick's throat no longer troubled him. He had not given a thought to the killings until they had driven back over the divide that separated Gold Hill and Virginia City. Now, however, he wondered if there would be a crowd waiting for them and if he would be asked a lot of dumb questions by Sheriff Nye.

Nye was a good man, though Rick's father hated him for being so officious. Because he was also Mandy's father, there had been a time years ago when Rick had wondered if Sheriff Nye might someday become his father-in-law. Now, that possibility was completely out of the question. Jenny French was going to be his woman. She was exactly what he needed and more than he had ever expected.

"What are you going to say to your father?"

"I'll tell him you're quitting him."

"He'll get mad as hell," Jenny said, her brows knitted with worry. "I . . . well, you know that I was earning him a lot of money."

"That's history," Rick said. "It's done. I don't want to talk about it ever again."

Jenny hugged his neck. "Where are we going to live?"

"Upstairs."

"In the Silver Dollar?" Jenny was unable to hide her disappointment.

"Sure, why not?"

"Couldn't we live someplace else?"

"No," he said. "It's where I have my room. It's free and it's convenient."

"Well, what am I supposed to do now?"

Rick had not given that any thought. He supposed that Jenny could not simply sit around all day waiting for him to take her out. "I'll think of something," he said. "Can you sing or dance?"

"Not professionally."

"Can you sing at all?"

"Well, of course. Everyone can sing some."

"Then I'll hire you a teacher," Rick said. "He'll give you voice lessons and teach you how to sing well enough to accompany the saloon piano. As pretty as you are, we'll pack the house every night."

Jenny cocked her head to one side. "I think we just might," she said after a few moments' deliberation. "I sort of like the idea, too."

"Good! Then it's all settled."

Jenny pointed to the Silver Dollar. "Isn't that Sheriff Nye and your father standing there?"

"It sure is," Rick said. "I was afraid of this. I'm going to have to answer some questions."

When he drove up, Nye and Ulysses were arguing loudly. Ulysses was obviously outraged that anyone would be stupid enough to question his son for killing two men in self-defense in front of dozens of witnesses.

"Dammit!" Nye swore. "It's just for the record. Hello, Rick."

Rick nodded in return, then said, "Pa, I don't mind answering a few of Sheriff Nye's questions."

"*I* mind! We're responsible citizens, and you and your lady friend were attacked right out in the open. Dozens of people saw it happen, and if I hadn't been half asleep, I'd have shot them bastards myself. Shot 'em in the belly so they'd wriggle around in the dirt and die thinking about the bad mistake they made."

Sheriff Nye was pale-complected and now he flushed with anger. He was smaller than Ulysses but very expert with both fists and guns, and he was not a man to be taken lightly. "I don't see any sense in that kind of talk," he told Ulysses. "I don't like it."

"Sheriff, what you like or don't like don't concern me one damn bit. But you ain't takin' Rick to the jail and askin' him a hundred stupid questions."

"I have no choice," the sheriff said, his chin jutting out stubbornly. "The Storey County commissioners, the men who hire me, have made out a form I have to complete for every killing. It's just a formality, but I'm goin' to do 'er—rather you like it or not."

The two men glared at each other until Rick hopped down from the buggy and said, "Pa, I'll answer the sheriff's questions. I don't mind."

"Neither do I," Jenny said.

"Good," Nye said, turning to leave before there was any more argument. "You and Miss French can both come along then. You'll be finished within fifteen minutes."

Rick took Jenny's arm and brushed by Ulysses. "Just let it be," he said. "The sheriff is just doing his job."

Ulysses cursed softly and wheeled around on his heels and entered the saloon. "Drinks on the house! Tonight, we're celebratin' my boy becoming a real man! And anybody who don't think he's a chip off this old block had better think again."

When they came to the sheriff's office, Mandy and Ben were standing in wait. Mandy just nodded at him and stared at Jenny, but Ben said, "I just wanted you to know that I didn't go crazy down in the mine. It wasn't half bad."

This day had been so eventful that Rick had forgotten all about Ben and the Lucky Eagle Mine. He felt ashamed and guilty because it seemed like ten years ago since they had gotten tipsy yesterday up on Sun Mountain.

Mandy looked at Rick. "I'm sorry you had to kill two men today."

"They left me no choice."

Mandy started to say one thing, changed her mind and said, "So I've heard."

A brittle silence formed between them until Rick said, "Jenny, we'd better go inside and answer those questions."

Without waiting for an answer, he took Jenny's hand and went into the office, closing the door behind him.

"It's changed him," Mandy said with an edge to her voice.

Ben did not understand. "What is that supposed to mean? He's always practiced with a gun. He's been teaching me to use one so I'm almost as good."

"You'll never be as good at killing as Rick," Mandy said. "And if you ever do have to kill, I doubt you'll get into a wagon and go for a picnic as if nothing happened."

"What else should he have done?" Ben demanded. "Just sat around and felt bad all day?"

Mandy stared him right in the eye. "No, but you or my father wouldn't have felt like having fun after killing two men. Admit it."

Ben was confused. "I never killed a man so I just don't know how I'd feel afterward."

"You'd feel terrible," Mandy said. "And that's what makes you different from the Kilbanes of this world."

Ben did not want to think about it anymore. Something *had* changed. Maybe in himself more than in Rick. All he knew for sure was that he would never quite be able to view Rick in the same light with two notches on his sixgun. And there was the matter of Jenny French. The way they'd touched and looked at each other, well, it caused Ben to blush and at the same time to feel envy for them both. One thing for sure, he'd just bet they'd done more than eat and swim down at the Carson River. Maybe later, he'd think on it some, but right now, with Mandy, he was too embarrassed to think of it at all.

"Can I walk you home?" he asked.

"Thank you, but I'll wait for my father. He'll be along soon."

Ben shoved his hands in his pockets and tried to hide his disappointment. "Like I was saying earlier, I'm earning four dollars a day in the mines. That's a lot of money."

"Yes, it is," she said. "That's more than my father makes as sheriff."

Her terse statement caught him off guard. "It shouldn't be," he said. "Your father risks his life every day, same as we do down below."

"Sheriffs are always underpaid," Mandy said. "But it's the only thing he wants to do. It drove my mother away. I wouldn't be married to a sheriff for anything, but a good one like my father should be enshrined along with the saints."

Ben swallowed loudly. "What about a miner? I mean, would you ever marry one of them someday?"

Her expression softened and she touched his sleeve before she looked up into his eyes. "I don't know, Ben. It's a hard, dangerous job. I just think there ought to be better ways for a smart, ambitious man to spend his life. And I mean that as no disrespect for your father."

Ben suddenly felt miserable. It sounded to him as if Mandy was turning away from him and that, coupled with his troubled feeling about Rick, just made for too much all at once. He'd thought perhaps he and Mandy might go for a walk or something. And even if she had refused him, Rick had promised to buy him a drink with the other men at the Silver Dollar. But hell, neither one of those things was going to happen now.

"I guess I better go along home," he said. "We start early in the morning."

"Yes," Mandy said. "I know. Congratulations. I'm very proud of you for going down there and I'll bet your father is too."

Ben managed a smile. "Thanks," he said as he turned and walked away feeling lower than a centipede.

CHAPTER FOUR

Ben had not slept at all that night, wondering how he was going to avoid his promotion into the farthest reaches of the mine. Earlier in the week, he had almost worried himself sick every time the cage had come down because he knew it might carry his station attendant replacement. And then, two days ago, it had happened. A young Irishman named Sean O'Doyle had come down grinning and happy as could be.

"I'll be taking over here day after tomorrow," he'd said happily, "so I want to know everything you do. I mean to be earning five dollars a day with the other miners just as soon as I can. Got a wife and a baby to take care of, you know."

Ben had nodded woodenly and then he'd gone about showing O'Doyle all the supplies and how to order them and keep up the ice, and most important of all, how to use the signal bell to pass messages up and down the deep shaft so that the hoisting operator knew exactly when to raise or lower a cage to their station.

"Is that all there is to it, now?"

"It's damned important!" Ben had snapped. "Make one mistake and someone might get crushed by the cage. You cannot be daydreaming when you touch that signal bell!"

O'Doyle had taken offense at his tone of voice, but Ben did not give a damn. He resented O'Doyle for putting him into this fix, even though it was not the Irishman's fault. They had spoken to each other only when required and yesterday afternoon it was easy to see that O'Doyle had already considered himself in charge of things and was competent to take over.

Long before daylight, Ben heard his father's snoring stop and then, a few minutes later, he heard the familiar creaking of the floor as George padded across the two-room shack. The man stepped outside in the darkness and urinated. He grunted, stepped back inside and groped for a kerosene lamp which he lit and which drenched the cabin in light. "Time to get up, son," he said, running his hands through his thinning hair. "Today's important."

Ben did not move at first. He stared up at the bare rafters and tried to summon up the courage to admit to his father that he was scared of being inside close places. He'd always been scared of close places, but now he was going to be herded into one, whether he liked it or not.

"Pa," he said, not taking his eyes off the rafters. "Pa, I was wondering if you'd mind if I stayed on my job at the station."

"What!"

George Pope was suddenly very wide awake now. "Get up, you!" he said in anger. "What kind of talk is that, now!"

Ben's mind froze and he stammered, "It's . . . it's just that I was thinking . . ."

"Ah," his father said, pointing a finger in his face. "You was thinking about Sean O'Doyle and his family. And how that extra dollar a day would help him out. Well, yes, it would, but we need the money as well. Sean will get his turn."

"Yeah, but . . ."

"I won't hear another word of it," George said. "The talking is over. Get dressed and we'll eat a bite and go."

Ben nodded, feeling as if he were helplessly caught in some

tragedy that must be played out to the bitter end. He swung his legs and planted his feet on the floor, then reached for his pants.

Maybe he would be all right. Maybe it wouldn't be so bad. Maybe he would not disgrace himself and panic in the close, hot mine tunnels that riddled the entire Comstock.

Maybe, but not very damn likely.

When the cage delivered Ben into the steamy hell of the twelve-hundred-foot-level station, Sean O'Doyle was already at work. He was whistling happily and stopped when he saw Ben to say, with a new air of propriety, "I'm in charge here now, but I'll be following along after you in a month, so save some hard rock for me to tackle."

Ben said nothing in acknowledgment as his eyes panned around the station at the now familiar boxes of supplies, the huge barrel of water that he had fed ice, the tables and the cups that he had cleaned for the shift after their rest and meal breaks. And then, he stared at the main drift down which he was expected to go this morning with his father and the others.

A drift was called a tunnel when its mouth opened on the surface. Under Virginia City, it paralleled the main vein of ore, north and south on the Comstock Lode. The main drift was only about eight feet in diameter, with a car track running right down its center which led from the crosscuts to the cage where the ore carts were lifted to the surface.

Ben had stood poised at the mouth of this particular drift many times during this past month, but he had never entered it because its close presence gave him a choking feeling.

"Get yourself a pair of gloves and three candles," George

said. "No time to stand gawking. We're expected to haul out ten carts filled with ore on this shift and that means we have to bust our backs."

"I'll do my best," Ben said, moving woodenly across the station and selecting the candles and a pair of gloves.

George said, "Son, you're mighty quiet this morning, you feel all right?"

"I feel a little sick," Ben admitted, a spark of hope rising that he could be excused and prolong the inevitable show-down with his inner demons one more day.

"You'll feel better once we get in there and get to work," George said. "Before we start, though, I want you to know that this is a proud day in my life and that of your mother. She's worked too damn hard these past few years and now that she has two men to care for her, things are gonna be fine. Next week, I thought we'd even pick her out a dress and a new hairbrush. What do you think?"

"I'd like that," Ben said, unable to tear his eyes off the mouth of the drift. "How far back will we be working?"

"Huh?"

"How far in there will we go?"

"About eight hundred yards is all. We'll be on this level for another six months at least. Let's go."

George followed the other miners into the drift. Because the heat and smoke given off by the kerosene lamps fouled the already bad air, the men held candles in small iron holders that could be wedged into beams or even into the crevasses of rock so that they could see while they worked.

Ben stepped into the drift, then paused. The sense of being crushed and smothered assailed his senses so forcibly that he

reached out and touched the warm rocks and steadied himself.

George and the other miners were leaving him behind and
Ben knew that his absence would soon attract their attention.
He concentrated on the iron tracks and moved forward, his
candle held out before him to illuminate the drift. Almost at
once, he had the awful sensation that the drift had closed in
behind him and he was buried alive. His breath came faster
and the smoke from his candle seemed to swirl panic into his
frenzied mind.

"Steady," he whispered to himself. "Steady!"

But he could not be "steady" and his hand betrayed him as
the candle bounced up and down at the end of his arm. Still
he pushed on, hearing the voices up ahead and taking some
comfort in their easy banter, a bark of laughter, already the
sound of a pick striking and dropping ore to be loaded into
the carts.

Ben moved faster. He knew that he was walking alongside
the greatest body of ore that the world ever discovered. Surprisingly, the silver and gold was not, even in its purest form, a
glittering mass but instead, it was bluish-gray or even deep
black. The sulphuret ore had a slightly metallic luster, and
occasionally, even a pale green cast.

What did glitter were the thick veins of quartz and iron
pyrites. Ben came to a dogleg in the drift, and when he
rounded the corner, he almost gasped with amazement as the
walls of the tunnel sparkled like diamonds. Huge quartz crys-
tals hung from the ceilings, and when his pale candlelight
touched their millions of faceted surfaces, the colors surpassed
anything Ben imagined could have existed.

"Ben, come on!" his father shouted from somewhere up ahead.

Ben hurried onward. His heart was pounding and he was sweating even more than would be expected in the terrible heat. At last, he passed the first group of men working a crosscut into the vein. They had stripped off their shirts, and while one man beat at the wall and ceiling with a pick and brought ore down, the other worked hard to load it into a waiting ore cart with its own short track leading into the crosscut.

Ben stopped and stared at the two miners who were completely oblivious to his presence. In the flickering candlelight, with pyrite and quartz gleaming all about them, they seemed ethereal, things of another world. Stripped to the waist, covered with a sheen of perspiration, their bodies radiated an unnatural whiteness.

One suddenly looked up. "What are you standing there staring at us for!" he snapped. "Get to work and earn your pay!"

Ben stumbled on passing more crosscuts and straining miners. All up and down the drift he could hear the sounds of men grunting with exertion as picks struck rock and rock fell to strike the floor. Each rock was lifted and then dropped heavily into the squat iron ore carts which banged and visibly shuddered on their tracks.

At last, he reached the crosscut where his father worked. "What the hell have you been doing!" George demanded. "Start loading that rock!"

Ben reached down and began to scoop up the loose rock his father had already broken off the wall and the crosscut. He threw the rock into their cart and reached for more until he had it all cleared out of the drift. His father was swinging his pick with a steady rhythm that he could sustain for hours.

"You watch me when you're not loading rock," George panted. "Watch how I work both the face of this crosscut and then its ceiling. I move up and down, and then from right to left. Never varies. Keep your head down when the pick bites or you'll blind yourself right away. Look for fissures and wet spots which tell you there might be a scalding reservoir of water you don't want to tap. I've seen men boiled standing upright."

George glanced back at his son. He was still angry that Ben had held back and caused them a late start. There was catching up to do. "You listening to me!"

"Yes sir!"

Ben concentrated everything he had on loading the cart as fast as possible. He did not look up or sideways, only down, as he rushed to grab each rock. The sound of his father's pick matched his own heartbeat, and when the car was finally loaded, he kept throwing rock up and onto it until it began to cascade back to the floor.

"Hey!" George shouted. "Look what you're doin'! The cart is so full you'll never even be able to push it back to the station."

The station!

"I can push it!" Ben grabbed his candle and threw himself at the ore cart. It creaked forward and he got low and drove his right shoulder into it, his legs knotting and the toes of his work boots scratching for purchase as the cart slowly edged onto the drift track.

"You'll kill yourself doing that," George said. "Take some off!"

But Ben did not hear his father. The blood was pounding in his ears and the cart was gaining momentum. He did not dare stop it now, and already it was leaving the crosscut behind.

"Hey!" George shouted.

Ben kept driving the cart along, and then, he slipped. The toes of his work boots caught on the track and he fell, slamming his forehead against the lip of the cart and knocking his candle to the floor where it died.

Instantly, he was plunged into almost total darkness. Dazed and with blood pouring down into his sightless eyes, horror rose in his throat like a gorge and he began to choke as the blackness smothered his reason.

"Ahhhh!" he screamed, jumping to his feet and running blindly into the wall. "Ahhhh!"

He heard voices, saw flickering lights up ahead and panic drove him forward. Someone tried to grab him, but his terror gave him inhuman strength and he knocked them aside as if they were made of papier-mâché.

Ben could not stop running and screaming. The sounds of his madness filled the drift. He forgot about the dogleg and ran upright into a beam. He was knocked almost witless to the floor but scrambled erect and staggered on until the light of the station filled the round hole of the drift.

Ben threw himself into it like a man bursting up from a grave.

"Jesus Christ!" Sean O'Doyle screamed. "Jesus Christ, what is wrong!"

Blood streaming down his face, his eyes wild and rolling, Ben charged headlong toward the waiting cage and grabbed the bellpull which he began to yank.

"Hey, stop that!" O'Doyle yelled. "Get out of there!"

The Irish station attendant tried to grab his arm, but Ben doubled up his fist and hit him so hard that O'Doyle was lifted completely off his feet and went skidding across the floor.

Ben looked up the shaft. It was so far to the surface that he could not even see a light. But he knew it was up there somewhere. "Come on!" he cried. "Come on!"

In answer, he felt the cage shiver with anticipation. The hoisting operator far overhead had received his message. Any moment the cage would swoop upward.

"Ben!"

He looked to see his father come bursting out of the drift followed by the rest of the shift. "Get out of there, Ben!"

Ben gripped the cage and shook his head. "Stay back!"

But George was filled with a desperation of his own making. He could not fathom or forgive a son who would run from his duty. Plowing forward, he grabbed Ben and tried to tear him from the cage.

Ben reared back and smashed him in the face. Once, twice, and the second time he heard his father's nose pop and saw blood gush over his mouth, chin and chest.

George staggered backward. "Coward!" he screamed. "You goddamn no-good coward! You're no son of mine!"

Ben turned his back on his father and all the rest of them. They would have to chop off his hands to make him release the cage. Somewhere high above he heard the mine cable snap and then he felt the cage leap off the station floor and carry him upward faster than any bird ever flew.

Great sobs racked his body and he tasted blood, but he did not dare to wipe it even from his eyes until the cage jerked and then bounced up and down at the top of the shaft.

"What the . . ."

Ben threw himself off the cage and charged past the surprised workmen until he found the door. Running like a man possessed, he headed straight for the gate.

"Stop!" one of the guards yelled. "Stop for the search!"

But Ben had no intention of stopping, and when the guards finally realized that and tried to grab him, he lowered his broad shoulders and knocked them both to the ground.

One of the guards yanked his shotgun upward, but the other slapped it back down. "You gonna shoot a boy that went crazy!"

"But he might have took some ore!"

"No, he didn't. Look at him run! I tell you, he went crazy down below. I seen it happen once before."

The guard shoved his gun back into his holster and brushed the dirt from his uniform. "Wasn't that George Pope's boy? The one that he bragged was going to make the best miner on the Comstock?"

"Yeah, but I'll bet he ain't braggin' no more. Not after this day!"

The other guard nodded as they both watched the tall, powerful young man disappear up the hill toward Virginia City.

Ben sat very still while Jenny French cleaned the gash across his forehead and Rick stood watching with an expression of deep concern.

"You really should have this sewn up by a doctor," Jenny said. "Otherwise, it will leave a scar just under your hairline."

"I don't care." Ben gripped a glass of whiskey, and even though it had been refilled twice, his voice still held a tremor.

"You were right, Rick. I should have told Pa from the start. It couldn't have gone worse this morning, even if I'd planned it."

"Give him a few days," Rick said. "He's your father. He'll come around."

"No, he won't," Ben said. "As far as he's concerned, I'm dead and he has no son. He said as much and I know him better than anyone. Me becoming a miner was the most important thing in his life."

Rick sighed. "It shouldn't have been. Your father has to understand that everyone is different. Besides, he's seen enough men die in the mines to know it's no good."

"It's his whole world. He takes pride in mining and I shamed him."

"Then to hell with him!" Rick said angrily. "You couldn't help it that you were born afraid of being closed in! It wasn't something you made happen just so you could rain on your father's damned parade. *It isn't your fault!*"

"He's right," Jenny said. "Your father was wrong to treat you as he did."

"I shamed him," Ben repeated, drinking steadily. "And I let Ma down too."

Rick was getting upset. "What you're doing is filling yourself up with whiskey and pity. That won't help. What you need to do is to wait a few days and then go on down to your shack and explain things. Tell him you're sorry, if that will make you feel better. Offer to shake his hand, and if he refuses, then turn your back on him and walk away."

Jenny finished cleaning and bandaging the gash across his forehead. "You're too handsome to have that scar."

"I don't care about my looks," Ben said.

Rick walked over to his friend. "Well maybe you don't, but what about Mandy Nye? Maybe she liked you better when you didn't look like some Indian tried to peel your scalp back. Come on, let's go see Doc Whitman."

"Naw."

Rick was clean out of patience. He grabbed his friend and hauled him to his feet. "You better come," he said, "because from the way you look right now, I can sure as hell whip you."

"All right," Ben said, "in that case, I guess I will come along."

It was five days later when Ben finally screwed up his resolve and decided to see his parents. He didn't figure that his pa would ever speak to him again and he might even want to fight, but at least he had to see and explain things to his mother. She had to understand why he'd broken his father's nose with his fist and then run away.

Ben took a bath, dressed in new clothes that Rick had bought for him and then combed his hair neatly down over the heavy bandage that was wound around his head.

"You look fine," Jenny said with approval. "And I'll bet that your pa feels as bad as you about what happened down in the mine. He's probably thinking that there are better ways to make a living for his son than being a miner."

Ben did not believe what she said. Still, it was possible and he was determined to try and explain to his parents how he had felt in the drift and why he had acted like a crazy man.

"Wave to Rick as you go out the door and just remember, he's promised you a job as a swamper and it could lead to something a whole lot better someday. You're Rick's blood brother."

"So he told you about that."

"He sure did. He also says you're the best friend that he's got. Me, I'm the best woman he's ever gonna have."

Ben turned at the door. "You really love him. I mean, you're not just here because of his money or anything."

"No, it isn't the money," she answered, "but don't tell him that."

Instead of smiling as she'd hoped, Ben looked so sad that Jenny rushed over and kissed his cheek. "It'll be all right," she said quietly. "Just tell 'em the truth."

Once downstairs, Ben waved on his way out of the Silver Dollar and Rick started to get up from the roulette table he was running, but Ben hurried outside. Jaw set with determination, he hurried up C to Taylor Street, made a right turn at the corner and kept moving up the hill until he came to Howard Street where he turned left and didn't stop until he came to his house.

It wasn't much of a house at all. Just a shack, really, one no better or worse than the others surrounding it. His mother had planted a small garden and some flowers, but the earth was so poor and rocky that neither grew very well.

Ben halted beside the gate, and even before he entered it, he knew something was wrong. Then it hit him. There were no clothes hanging on the long washlines that his mother used. Her flowers were wilted and the house looked very still.

"What are you doin' here at a time like this!"

Ben whirled to see Mrs. Dorriety standing behind him with her hands resting on her skinny hips, wearing a look of utter contempt. She was a pinch-faced old widow with the sharpest tongue in the neighborhood and he'd feared her from the moment his family had moved in next door to her on this street.

"Where are they?" he asked.

The woman was wearing a faded dress that clung to her shrunken flesh. She was hatless. Her white hair was a bird's nest and her socks were rolled close down around her dirty ankles. "You know where she is! At the cemetery! Same place you ought to be, seein' as you're the one that killed him."

Ben reached out and grabbed the rickety gate. "Pa . . . he's dead?"

"Deader'n a snake, thanks to you!"

Ben lunged forward and grabbed the old woman by her bony shoulders. "What do you mean, 'thanks to me!' " he cried. "I didn't kill him."

"Take your dirty hands offa me, you coward!"

Ben shoved the woman away from him, then whirled and ran up Howard Street to Sutton where he turned right. He followed Sutton down to D Street and didn't stop running until he came to the huge wrought-iron gate and fence that protected the dead from digging coyotes. He entered the gate when he saw his mother sitting alone beside a fresh grave.

Pa *was* dead.

"Ma?"

She looked up at him, her face grief-stricken, and he wondered if she would run him off or throw her arms around his neck and cry.

"Why?" she asked. "Why did you break his heart?"

"I couldn't help it," he choked, unable to tear his eyes from the fresh grave.

She nodded. "After that, he got drunk and then he decided

he was going to go down in the mine and work double shifts
—to make up for you."

Ben clenched his hands until the knuckles were white.

"He fell—or jumped off the cage." Her red-rimmed eyes
bored into his face. "It doesn't matter. There wasn't enough
pieces of him to fill a flour sack. He . . ."

She bit her lip and turned away. "I'm going to New York
City," she said in a hard voice. "Your aunt is the only person I
know who can help me."

"*I* can help you! We can leave here and never come back.
I'll take you to California and we'll farm and . . ."

"Farm! We're a *minin'* family. We don't know nothin'
about farmin'! You're crazy."

"I *need* to help!"

"No!" she cried, shaking his hand off her arm. "You've
done enough already! Now leave us alone!"

Ben climbed to his feet. He wanted to say something, but
the words wouldn't come and so he just walked away. He
wanted to find a gun or a bottle of whiskey, and it didn't
much matter to him which came first.

CHAPTER FIVE

Jenny French baked Rick a chocolate cake on his twenty-first birthday and Ulysses bought a hundred cases of French champagne. That night before a packed house, he gave Rick a full partnership in the Silver Dollar Saloon and the drinks were on the house for everyone who came in the door—everyone, that is, except Ben Pope.

It was close to midnight and it was snowing outside when Rick saw his old friend shamble out of a snowstorm dressed as raggedly as a scarecrow. Rick, Jenny, Ulysses and a few of the girls were sitting around a big table when Rick stood up so quickly that he almost knocked their champagne glasses over.

"Rick, no!" Jenny cried, seeing the way his eyes flashed with anger.

But Rick was already moving across the crowded saloon floor and men were stepping aside to create a path between him and Ben Pope. When Ben saw Rick coming at him, he already had a glass of champagne in his hand and he tossed it down, his face reddening as he straightened.

"Get out of here," Rick said. "I told you never to come back in here unless you were sober and were asking for sarsaparilla."

Ben wiped his nose with the back of his sleeve, then brushed the snow from his hair. He was shivering and his nose ran. He wasn't quite drunk yet, but he certainly wasn't sober and he had changed a great deal in the five years since the death of his father. His once powerful shoulders were now thin and his face was haggard and drawn. "I guess you figure your old blood brother isn't worth inviting to your little birthday party."

"Not anymore, he isn't."

"You want to try and throw me out this time, or am I going to have a bottle of your French on the house?" Ben asked, looking from Rick to the bartender. "One for *my* birthday next month."

Rick's jaw muscles corded and he took a half step forward, but then he stopped when Ben balled his big fists up and said, "I can't be hurt anymore. You can't whip me, not even if I go down to stay."

The fight drained out of Rick. "No," he said quietly, "I guess you're the only one that can destroy yourself. And you're doing a pretty good job already."

He nodded to the bartender. "Give him a full bottle."

Ben relaxed. "Thanks," he said, without any warmth. "If I get drunk enough, might be I'll climb on a horse and then break my neck like Old Virginny who christened this hell-town."

"Maybe so," Rick said. "Or throw yourself down a mine shaft like your father. Either way, it's cleaner and quicker than drinking yourself to death."

"Yeah," Ben said. He looked across the room. "Ulysses and Jenny still mad at me?"

"Stay away from them," Rick ordered. "My pa has a short fuse. You left a lot of ill will the last time you quit on us."

"Cleaning spittoons wasn't much fun."

"It was work," Rick said. "The only work you were able to do."

Their eyes locked and then Ben shook his head. He took the bottle that was placed before him, raised it in toast and said, "Happy birthday, blood brother."

Then he walked out the door and down the street with a fixed smile on his lips. He stood for a moment on the snowy boardwalk and took another drink, feeling the warmth of the champagne seeping from his gut toward his extremities. It wasn't much of a Sierra storm. The wind was light and capricious, big snowflakes were spinning in the air and he watched them cross the light from the saloon.

Ben was not sure where he wanted to go now that he had more to drink than he'd dared hope. He knew that he was not welcome anywhere, not even the stable where old Denton Tucker had let him sleep for the past few weeks in exchange for cleaning stalls. Ben stepped out into the street and gazed up at the sky. There was enough light from the saloons and other businesses along C Street so that it was real pretty to watch the snowflakes. The storm that had brought this December snowfall appeared to be breaking up and he could see the moon struggling through the clouds.

His eyes raised to the top of Sun Mountain and as always when he thought of its peak, he was reminded of the day he had graduated from high school and then gotten slightly drunk with Rick. He remembered how they had talked about things, though he forgot exactly what things, and how Rick had laughed when he'd fallen down the steep trail. Rick had given him a new shirt and pants, but they'd long since been worn out and thrown away.

On a crazy whim, Ben decided that he might as well climb

back up to the top of Sun Mountain and spend the night. Maybe up there, he'd be above the clouds and the swirling snow. He could drink his precious champagne in peace and watch the moon and the stars glide around in the heavens.

Shoving the bottle into his dirty coat pocket, Ben headed up King Street, walking with a purpose for the first time in as long as he could remember. Approaching the King Mansion, he heard piano music and a woman singing the ballad "The Streets of Laredo." It was one of Ben's favorites and he halted to peer up through the big windows of the mansion and wonder if Mandy Nye were inside and if he was listening to her sweet voice.

When the song ended, he heard applause and then laughter. A couple stepped up to the window and happened to look down into the street. For a moment, their faces were happy and then the girl's smile died and Ben staggered back to see that it really was Mandy. Their eyes locked with one another and then the young man pulled Mandy aside.

Ben swung away and continued up the mountainside. Leaving the city, he followed the ridge trail steadily upward, sometimes slipping and falling, but always careful not to break the bottle of champagne. When he finally reached the crest of Sun Mountain, he sat down very carefully on a rock and gazed down at Virginia City. The lights of the city glittered like the quartz and pyrite he had seen that last day in the Lucky Eagle Mine.

Ben drew his bottle out of his coat and took a long pull and then another. The inner warmth that had been lost while climbing began to seep back into his extremities and he wished that Mandy would sing again. Despite the wind, her voice might carry up to him and her singing, coupled with the champagne and the glittering lights of the city, would make it a very nice birthday party after all.

But Mandy's sweet voice was not to be heard again, and after a while the champagne made him sleepy and the lights of Virginia City began to fade.

"Ben! Wake up! Ben!"

He felt his head being rocked back and forth by the force of steady blows, but there was no pain and he did not open his eyes, much preferring to go back to his wonderful dream. It was summertime and he was with Mandy. They were standing chest-high in a field of corn and they could see the great Sacramento River, whose water was giving their fields life.

"Jesus Christ, is he dead!" Rick cried.

"No," Mandy said, "I can still feel a pulse. But we've got to get him down from here! The storm is getting worse."

"I'll drag him down if I have to. Maybe that will wake him up."

"It will kill him."

"That's what he wants, isn't it!"

Ben saw the vision of Mandy and his fields blur, and then he felt himself being roughly pulled to his feet. He opened his eyes and saw Mandy in the moonlight. Her hair was covered with snow and she looked like a frozen angel. He tried to say something to her, but all thought of conversation ended when he was dumped over Rick's shoulder. He felt Rick moving under him, and then he closed his eyes and went back to sleep.

When he awoke, Rick was gone, but Mandy was still with him and the sun was shining through a bedroom window. "Where am I?" he whispered, looking down at a thick layer of blankets that covered him.

"You're in Mrs. Nettie Walker's house," she answered. "She's taken you in for a while. I promised her that you would never drink again as long as you stayed here."

"You shouldn't make promises I can't keep."

"You're going to be dead soon if you don't stop drinking," she said to him. "And you're too young and fine a man to die."

"You and Rick should have left me alone up there."

"Maybe I should have," Mandy said. "But when I saw your face as you stood out in the street . . . I felt so terrible that I began to cry. I couldn't stop crying, Ben."

He turned away, feeling sure that she was going to start crying right now, and if that happened, he would cry with her and they would both be ashamed of themselves.

"The young man I was with—Mitchell Todd, he's the assistant manager of the bank."

"I've never had the pleasure of his acquaintance," Ben said. "I do my personal banking elsewhere."

She shook her head. "I'll bet you do. Anyway, he was very concerned about me, but I asked him to take me to see Rick. He was even more concerned. I told Rick I had a feeling inside that you were going somewhere to freeze to death. Rick left his birthday party and came. It was easy to follow your tracks. No one else would be climbing that mountainside in a storm."

"Where did he go afterward?"

"I don't know." Mandy looked puzzled. "Probably back to his saloon and Miss French. It doesn't matter. All that matters is that we helped you when you needed help. And now, you have to be good—for the rest of your life."

"Why?" Ben demanded. "Give me one good reason why."

Mandy thought about that. "Because," she said slowly, "last night on the way down from the mountain, you said you wanted to have a farm in California."

"What else did I say?" he asked, afraid that he'd also told her about the role she had always played in his dream.

"You said that I was going to be your wife and we would be happy."

"Oh, damn," he groaned. "I was afraid of that. I'm sorry to have insulted you."

"I was flattered to death," she said, reached down and turned his face toward her. "I have watched you suffer so long that, until the moment our eyes touched through the window last night, I'd erased the memory of how you used to smile, and act. You used to be the class clown. You were funny then. I never laughed so hard as when you were being funny."

Ben felt his eyes sting. "Now I'm just a clown. Mandy, I think I'd like to be alone and sleep a little while now."

"Of course." And then Mandy did a strange and wonderful thing, she reached down and kissed his cheek before she left his bedside.

At the door, she turned and said, "You're going to love Nettie. She'll fatten you up and make you smile. She's just what the doctor ordered, Ben. Together, we're going to make you want to live again."

"Another promise I can't keep."

"No," she told him, "a promise *I'll* keep."

During the next few days, Ben thought a lot about Mandy's promise when he was feeling well enough to think straight. He couldn't sleep at night and he felt terrible, with alternating sweats and chills so bad that he was either knotted up under his blankets or else wishing he could throw open his window and bolt out into the cold winter air.

Nettie Walker was in her seventies, at least. She had a big frame and soft, powder-blue eyes that looked as if they'd seen plenty of suffering of their own. Her hair was a washed-out gray color and she wore it tied in a severe bun. Nettie also had a mustache, but Ben didn't care. The woman was kind and she seemed to like him in her house.

"You're gonna be a big, strong boy when you get well again," she was often heard to say. "You must be what? Six-three or four?"

"Just six-one, Ma'am."

"Pushwash! You're taller than that! You're taller than Clyde used to be before he drank himself to death."

"Your husband, Ma'am?"

"Of course he was. The poor fool drank night and day for the first thirty-two years of our marriage. He quit, but the doc says he'd already ruined his health and he died five years ago. We had a good last few years though, good enough to balance out the first thirty-two."

"Was he a miner?"

"Nope. A freighter," she said. "And a fine one when he was sober enough to handle a team and a bullwhip. You ever think of becoming a freighter, young man?"

"No, Ma'am."

"Well, why not?"

"I don't like horses all that much."

"Humph! You must be crazy. I like horses better than men, and I like men a lot."

When Nettie smiled, her mustache would bristle and she'd show him that she was missing her two upper front teeth. The sight of her smiling made Ben feel good for some strange reason. It made him think that, if a woman as old and ugly as Nettie Walker could enjoy herself, why, he ought to be able to do about as well.

Nettie liked to tell him stories, too. She had been raised in Texas, seen Sam Houston and been living with Clyde and raising children and chickens when Santa Anna took the Alamo and his armies drove the Texans out.

"Sam Houston is my hero," she'd say. "He was sometimes drunk, but he was as great a man as there ever lived. Even greater than Abe Lincoln who got hisself assassinated a couple years ago. Bless their hearts. Houston saved Texas, but he should have shot that swine Santa Anna when he whipped him at San Jacinto. Only bad mistake he ever made. I saw Sam Houston a bunch of times."

"You did?"

"Yeah, and he was a big, big man. Bigger than you. Not as good-lookin' though," she added with a wink. "I liked to hear Sam laugh. He could laugh so loud that it'd shake the walls and make the candles flutter. I'd have gone after him myself if I hadn't already been married to Clyde."

"The Lord loves a faithful woman," Ben said.

"Where'd you hear that one?"

"I don't know. Maybe my mother said it once or twice. She used to read the Bible."

Nettie Walker was very interested in his mother and his father. She'd ask him all kinds of questions and then one day, she said, "You ought to find your mother someday and see if she needs your help."

"I'm in no position to help anyone," Ben said. "I don't even know how I can pay you for all this."

"The Lord will pay me some. There are others that will pay the rest."

"Rick Kilbane being one of them?"

"Maybe. Him and I get a little help from Mandy and her father."

"The sheriff!"

Nettie smiled. "Sheriff Nye says he's locked you up in jail a hundred times for being drunk and rowdy. He's got to feed you in jail and that costs the citizens of this town money. He figures it's cheaper in the long run to pay me a little money to keep you sober and out of trouble."

"Makes sense," Ben said, looking out the window and seeing the sun shining. "I'd like to get dressed and go for a walk."

"I got to find Mandy and see if she can go along with you," Nettie said.

Ben frowned. "I sure don't need any nursemaid to hold my hand. I've been walking around this town on my own for years."

"Staggering is more accurate." Nettie's eyes narrowed and her jaw seemed to push forward. "I seen you dozens of times. I'd say to myself, 'That there Pope boy is sure awastin' his young life. And such a big, handsome son he would be if he took some food instead of whiskey!' That's what I'd say to myself."

Ben had to grin. "Why don't you walk with me?"

"Can't," she said. "I got terrible feet. They pain me all the time and walkin' these steep hillsides is a torment."

"Then run next door and see if Mandy can go," Ben said as he eased out of bed. "If I'm to get strong, I need exercise."

"You need food and work," she said, heading for the door. "That's what you need."

A few minutes later, Ben stood by the door. They had washed his clothes and given him a new shirt. He'd bathed yesterday and shaved earlier, so he figured he looked just fine for Mandy and he was plenty eager to see her. She had not been around since early yesterday. As for Rick, well, he hadn't come by here at all and that was the purpose of the walk.

"Miss Mandy is out right now," Nettie said, looking at him. "You'll have to wait."

"No, I won't," Ben said. "I'm not a prisoner and I'm over my shakes. I guess I can go for a walk if I want to."

Nettie stepped in front of him and placed her heavily-veined hands on her broad hips. "You can," she said, "if you give me your word that you're not walkin' into a saloon."

"I can't do that," he said, seeing the consternation in her eyes. "But I'll promise you I won't take a drink of liquor. I'll take a sarsaparilla, and that's all."

"You mean that?"

"I do. I cross my heart I do."

When he made an elaborate cross on his chest, she relaxed and grinned, her mustache twitching. "I believe you, Ben. And I'm going to let you go."

"Thank you, Ma'am," he said, stepping around her. "Thank you very much."

He started down the road and she called, "Potato soup and fresh sourdough bread for supper. You be here in time."

"I will," he promised.

When he stepped into the Silver Dollar, he could feel the tension in the room and he'd been in enough saloons to recognize all the signs of a fight brewing. Normally, he had backed right out the door, but he needed to find Rick, so he hoped the fight would be with fists and not bullets as he headed toward the bar to ask the bartender where he might find Rick. But before he'd taken three steps, he heard an oath, and when he glanced back to the rear of the saloon, Ben saw four men move quickly away from a card table, leaving only two left to climb to their feet and glare at each other across a pile of chips and money.

"You sonofabitch!" Ulysses shouted. "You accuse me of usin' a marked deck. Fill your hand!"

The man, who was young and excited, looked down at the big stack of chips and money, then seemed to make his decision with a shake of his head. "Just forget I said that, Ulysses. I . . . I didn't mean it."

"Fill your hand," Ulysses growled. "Or die whinin'."

Ben stared as the man's fingers wiggled over his gunbutt. The room was deadly silent, and in the next heartbeat, the man stabbed for the butt of his gun. Ulysses hesitated just a split second so that it was clear he was drawing second, then his big Colt seemed to jump from his holster, level and fire in one smooth, continuous motion.

Ulysses pulled the trigger twice and each slug kicked the man before him back a half step. He was still trying to clear leather when he crashed into another table and knocked it over on its side. He slid down the table and did not move.

Ulysses studied him as one might a pesky insect that he had just squished. Looking around with his gun still in his big fist, he studied every single person in the Silver Dollar and then said, "Anybody gonna dispute the fact that I killed this sonofabitch in self-defense?"

Heads wagged. Everyone vowed they would not dispute the issue. No sir!

Ulysses was finally satisfied. "Right that table and bring a fresh bottle of whiskey over here for me and my friends. Pour drinks on the house!"

The bartender practically ran across the room with a bottle and glasses as Ulysses scooped up the money and yelled, "All right, let's go on with the game, dammit!"

Ben turned his back on the sight of fear and death, both of which he'd known and which he'd seen plenty of in his twenty-one years. He would say nothing, but there was something very wrong here. The young man who'd died had been forced to draw against a faster opponent. And he'd known he was going to get beaten and killed! Self-defense? Hardly. No matter what the law wanted to call it, Ben figured it had been murder.

The bartender scurried back behind the bar. He set up a row of glasses for the house and poured, spilling too much whiskey and rattling each glass, thus betraying his own fear.

Men reached for the whiskey, but Ben kept his hands at his sides, then turned his back on his poison and walked out the door. He could see Rick and thank him for saving his life up on Sun Mountain another time. Right now, he figured what he really needed, since drinking was impossible, was to see Mandy and maybe he would find her with Sheriff Nye.

When Ben entered the sheriff's office, he saw Mandy and her father and said, "I'm afraid there's been a shooting at the Silver Dollar Saloon, Mr. Nye."

The sheriff was a man of medium height and build, but he had a rugged face and a no-nonsense reputation. Nye was over forty, but he was still a force to be reckoned with, either in a fistfight or a gunfight. Few men who had seen him in a scrape cared to cross his path.

"Was it Ulysses Kilbane?"

"How'd you know?"

"Did you see the play?" Nye asked impatiently.

"I did."

"Describe it. Every word, every detail."

Ben glanced at Mandy, then as completely as was possible, he recounted what he'd seen and heard. As his account came to an end, the sheriff threw up his hands in exasperation. "And I don't suppose anyone thought or had the guts to ask to see those marked cards."

"No sir," Ben said. "It seemed to me that everyone just wanted to stay out of Ulysses' way."

The sheriff reached for his hat. "Of course they did. Ulysses Kilbane is a gunman, pure and simple. He's fast, and even more important, he's a treacherous old bastard. He won't brace another gunman without guaranteeing himself some kind of big edge."

Mandy said, "Father, do you have to go over there? I don't trust him anymore than you do!"

"I'll be all right," Nye said. "He knows I'm on a par with him when it comes to pulling a gun. Besides, he'll be drinking pretty strong already. No, he'll answer my questions right there in his saloon. I'll ask to see the damned marked deck they were playing with, and of course, the deck will have already been switched."

"I'll come along with you," Ben said.

"Why?"

Ben had not anticipated the question. He frowned and said, " 'Cause I can't think of anything better to do."

"You can stay right here and keep my nervous daughter company," Nye growled.

"I'd like to do that, but I think I still better come along."

Nye started to object, but Mandy said, "Please. Let him go along. I'll wait right here."

"Okay," Nye said. "But just keep your ears open and your mouth shut. If he tells me a lie, don't say a word until we get back here. You don't need Ulysses Kilbane as an enemy. Is that understood?"

"It is."

Sheriff Nye seemed satisfied and he said, "How many days you been sober now?"

"Almost a full week."

"You already look like a new man. Keep it up."

"I intend to, sir."

"Call me Sheriff or Frank, but not sir."

Ben nodded, looked back at Mandy and then followed the sheriff out the door. Though his were much longer legs, he had to hustle to keep up with the older man, and when he reached the Silver Dollar, Nye hesitated and said, "Remember, not a word."

During the next fifteen minutes, Ben had to keep reminding himself that he had promised to keep his mouth shut. It wasn't that Ulysses told big lies, it was just that he sort of stretched the truth beyond all recognition. He said that the man he'd killed had called him a cheat and to draw his gun or hand over the pot. That statement could only be verified by the other poker players, all of whom were conveniently on their way to Reno. Ulysses also said that the other man had drawn his gun first. Wrong! He'd been forced to *touch* his gun first. Hell, the poor devil hadn't even cleared leather!

By the time that Sheriff Nye was finished, Ben reckoned he'd had a real education as far as skillful lying was concerned.

"Hey!" Ulysses shouted as the sheriff walked away. "You, Ben Pope! Come on over here and have a drink with me. We need to talk."

"Don't do it," Nye said in a low voice out of the corner of his mouth as he walked past him and out the door.

"I got to go, Mr. Kilbane."

Ulysses came to his feet. "The hell you do! You got no job or nothin' to go to. Come on over here! Maybe I can help you out a little. Try you again cleanin' spittoons or something."

The bartender snickered. Ulysses leered and Ben swallowed his shame. "Find yourself another drunk," he stammered before he turned and walked out the door, hearing Ulysses and the others' laughter, and feeling it sting his soul.

CHAPTER SIX

Two days later, Ben was sitting in the sheriff's office as Frank Nye said, "The thing you have to remember is that you can't trust anyone when it comes to your own survival. For another, you need to remember that, when a man pins on a badge, he says that he intends to uphold the law, come hell or high water. And that means making the hard choices as well as the easy ones. Sometimes, you'll have to make a mighty unpopular arrest. Or investigate something others think ought to be better left alone. And if you find dirt, you can't just sweep it under the rug and pretend it isn't there."

The sheriff frowned. "Are you any good with a gun?"

"I used to practice with Rick Kilbane. Rick was fast, I was just so-so."

"So-so isn't necessarily all bad," Nye said. "More important than speed is coolness and accuracy under fire. There are a lot of slick hombres who can jerk a gun out quicker than a snake-strike. But there's damn few of 'em that can stand and fire with any kind of accuracy in a real fight."

"So how do you learn to be steady?"

"You don't," Nye said. "It either comes naturally or it doesn't. It helped me to always assume I was going to die in every gun battle."

"Are you serious?"

"Sure! Once you believe that, you begin to see that you

have nothing more to lose. And when there's nothing to lose, you don't get rattled."

"Hmmm," Ben mused. "That's a strange way of figuring it."

"Works for me," Nye said. "I've stood up against faster men that should have killed me but were too worried about dying to make their best draw."

Nye pulled a sixgun and holster out of his drawer. "This is one I took from Wild Ed Beechum. Remember him?"

Ben remembered with a nod. Wild Ed had been crazier than a loon and a dead shot. He'd killed five miners before the sheriff had tracked him down and followed him into a mine. When the shooting was over, the sheriff was the only one that came out alive.

"Everyone thought that Wild Ed didn't care if he lived or died. Not so! That man wanted very much to live. So much that he came apart when I cornered him. He drew first and fired three times before I drilled him in the gizzard. Just one bullet and it was over for Ed. Hell, I'd heard about his draw and I didn't even try to match it. All I wanted to do was to get one bullet fired, and that was enough."

The sheriff got up. "Here, take this and strap it on."

"Why?"

" 'Cause a man needs to know how to defend himself," the sheriff said. "Just strap it on and let's see how she hangs."

Ben strapped the gun on and raised his hands from his sides as the sheriff studied him, then said, "It's not loaded, draw and fire."

"I can't do that."

"Why the hell not?"

" 'Cause I'm all thumbs. My hands are too big and . . . well, I'd never be any good."

The sheriff raised his eyebrows. "Oh, I forgot. You're the young fella that has a dream of becoming a farmer and marrying my daughter. Gonna take her over to the Sacramento delta country and raise crops, is that it?"

Ben colored with embarrassment and said nothing.

The sheriff sat down on his desktop and swung one boot back and forth with agitation. "Even a farmer might have to defend himself. Remember John Sutter? He was a farmer back in the forties when Marshall discovered gold. Well, he was also a man who used words instead of weapons and look what words got him. Nothin' at all. As soon as the news reached San Francisco that gold was discovered, men rushed across Sutter's holdings like locust. They slaughtered his cattle and stole his crops right out of the fields. They squatted on his pastures and laughed at his hollow words."

"Are you saying that, if he had been good with a gun, he'd have saved his fortune?"

"I don't know," Nye admitted. "But he couldn't have done any worse than he did. And I'll bet that, if it had been my land, a few men would have gotten powder burns or else lead poisoning. At least I'd have gone down fighting for what was my own."

"What about the law?" Ben asked. "I thought it was the law that was supposed to protect one man's property from another man's greed."

Nye chuckled. "Clever of you to throw that right back at me, the local constable. But the truth—at least as clear as I can see the truth—is that a man can get hung by taking the law into his own hands. But at the same time, he stands a hell of a lot more chance of meeting some drunk or mean sonofabitch who will either humiliate him until he's got no manhood, or else kill him outright."

"So," Ben said, "you're telling me a man has to be able to protect himself and his property if the law isn't around."

"That's about the way of it, all right," Nye said. "So let's see if we can teach you a thing or two about handling a gun. Go ahead and draw, and then fire at that wall over there."

Ben turned to the back wall. It was made of heavy planking and was the rear wall of the cell. He took a deep breath, then his hand stabbed downward. The gunbutt felt too small and he had trouble getting his finger through the trigger guard, and when he finally did get the gun out and pulled the trigger, the gun boomed in his fist and damned near scared the wits out of him.

"You said it wasn't loaded!"

Nye grinned through the blue smoke. "I lied. When someone hands you a gun, *always* check for yourself to see if it's loaded and in good working order or not. *Never* take someone's word for something that your own life could depend upon. I told you that a few minutes ago, but you musta forgot. Are you going to remember the next time?"

Ben nodded. He was still smarting from the rude lesson.

"All right. Unload the gun and try it again."

Ben unloaded the cartridges and holstered the gun. He tensed, dropped his hand and made a grab for his gun, but Nye's fist clamped down on his wrist.

"Uh-uh," Nye said. "Don't tense up. Just relax and practice drawing, making pretend you were snatching flies out of the air."

"I never could snatch flies out of the air."

"*Pretend*, I said. Let your muscles stay loose and stand a little sideways. Once you fill out, you're going to be a large target. Put your right foot slightly in front of you, and when you bring the gun up, extend your arm straight out and fire from eye rather than hip level."

"But that'll be slower."

"Sure it will, but you've already shown me that you're not going to outdraw a really quick man, no matter how hard you practice."

"So what am I practicing at all for?"

"I've already explained that," Nye said. "We're just going to assume you are going to be a cool customer under fire and that you'll be able to convince yourself that you don't care if you live or die."

"What gave you the right to make that assumption?"

Nye looked him straight in the eye. "Hell, you've been drowning yourself in whiskey and self-pity for the last five years. That sounds to me like a man who doesn't care much about life."

Ben frowned. He reached for the gun on his hip, stuck his arm out and fired. "Things are getting better," he said.

"Maybe so, but they'll get a hell of a lot worse the day you decide to take my daughter to California and make her a damn farmer's wife."

Ben didn't know whether to laugh or get serious about that remark and he was saved from a decision when Rick Kilbane pushed open the door and saw him with his gun pointing at the wall.

Rick sniffed the air. "I thought I heard a gunshot as I was coming up the walk. It's a little close in here for a shooting lesson, isn't it, Sheriff?"

A mask dropped over Nye's face. "Yeah, I guess it is. Put it away, Ben. We'll try it again some other time."

"He'll never be as fast as you or me," Rick said. "He's built for strength, not quickness."

"So you both tell me," Nye said. "But there's a way to overcome every advantage or disadvantage. You just have to figure it out."

Rick studied him a minute, then turned his attention to Ben. "I understand you came into the saloon last week when my father was forced to defend his life. I was in Reno up until this morning, and I thought you might have come in to talk to me."

"I did," Ben said, looking from one man to the other and wondering why there was such a stiffness between them. He supposed that it was because Ulysses hated the sheriff and that meant that Rick would share at least some of those hard feelings. It was a shame.

"Since you're both here, I might as well thank you at the same time. I know you're paying Mrs. Walker for my keep and I want to say that I'll be getting a job one of these days soon and I'll repay each of you."

Rick's expression softened and he turned away from the sheriff. "I don't want repayment. And as for a job, that's one of the reasons that I came by. My father says he'll take you back on and it won't be to clean spittoons."

Ben grinned. "For a fact?"

"That's right. You'll be working in the storeroom and helping the bartenders keep the liquor stocked and the glasses washed. There's errands to run and . . ."

Sheriff Nye interrupted. "Ben is going to be working for me. I can use a deputy."

Ben twisted around. "What?"

"You heard me. I need someone to help out around here. You'll be watching prisoners and doing some paperwork. Once in a while I even need someone strong and willing to back me up when the odds get long. That's why I was teaching you how to use a gun."

"I already taught him," Rick growled. "And as for being a deputy, who's gonna pay him?"

"The city council has already okayed the money and given me free rein to hire whoever I choose. And I just chose Ben Pope."

"The city council won't let you hire a drunk."

"Ex-drunk," the sheriff said in a hard voice. "As you can well see."

Rick flushed with embarrassment. "I can see it and it's what I've been hoping to see for years. But it may not last and I don't think Ben needs the kind of pressure you'll put him under as a deputy. You've had deputies before and every one of them quit."

"Sure, to become sheriffs or marshals in some other town," Nye countered, with heat in his voice. "They learned how to do the job and they left to do it. I call that successful teaching."

The sheriff looked at Ben. "I know he's your blood brother and your best friend. I also know he's done a lot for you, but right now, what I'm offering is better. You don't need to be around Ulysses and a bunch of saloon folks."

"Now wait just a goddamn minute!" Rick shouted, coming forward. "You're way out of line."

"Maybe, maybe not," Nye said, standing up so that his hand was near his gun. "Either way, this is my office and I'll say whatever I want here. And while I'm on the subject of your father, let me say this—I aim to see him either strung up from a telegraph pole or sent to prison for the rest of his natural life. He's gotten away with murder time after time and it's going to end real soon."

Rick was trembling with rage. He raised his finger and said, "The day you come after my father, that's the day you had better come after me too."

"Thanks for the warning. I always figured you for just a younger, smarter version of the same rattler as Ulysses. And if you think about it, I've never turned my back on you either."

Ben could see the fury in their eyes and it made him sick with disappointment. Both were his friends, men who'd just saved his life and helped him start on the road to recovery and now, here they were threatening to kill each other.

He stepped between them, very much aware that Rick was wild enough to draw on the sheriff and take whatever consequences might come his way. Because Ben was still bigger than either man, he blocked their view of each other. "I think you'd both better cool off. Rick, thank your father for the job offer, but I guess I'll decline. Say hello to Miss French."

Rick stepped back. "Are you telling me that you're going to go to work for *him!*"

"I believe I will."

"After what he just said about me and my father? After what I've done for you!"

Ben stared at his hands. "Look at it this way," he said. "Maybe one of these days I can come between you and Sheriff Nye again and prevent something awful from happening. A bullet, or prison. Either one can kill you."

Rick was white with anger. "You're making a real bad mistake," he said. "One that you're gonna come to regret. You're betraying our friendship and I won't forget this."

Ben took a deep breath, then met Rick's eyes. "Yes, you will," he said. "Someday you'll see that I finally did the right thing."

"The hell you say," Rick snapped as he swung on his heel and barged out the door.

The sheriff waited a long time and then he said, "You surprised me just now. I think you're gonna make out fine."

Ben was staring at the door. "I owe Rick a lot. More than I owe anyone."

"You don't owe him a chance to make something of yourself," Nye said. "The last place you needed a job was in a saloon."

"That may be true, but you sure could find somebody better than me to back you up in a fight."

"Right now that's true. But Mrs. Walker is gonna fatten you up, and when your strength and size comes back, you're going to be a pretty big and imposing man. Me, I've always wanted to be tall and broad-shouldered like you, so that men would look at me and think twice about wanting to fight."

"People know your reputation and they don't want to fight you."

"Yeah, but it hasn't been easy. I've been whipped more times than I care to tell you. But I've also whipped some big and rough men. I'm getting too old for that stuff, though. And, if truth be known, I'm slowing down with a gun. Not so you or a miner would notice it, but Ulysses, now he'd notice."

"Ulysses is older than you are," Ben said. "And so he must have slowed even more, yet I saw his hand go for his gun and it was a blur."

"He's an amazing fella," Nye conceded. "The way he drinks and fornicates and raises hell over there, I'm surprised he isn't dead by now. But he's still one of the most dangerous men I've ever known and he's still killing folks to satisfy his blood lust. You saw it."

Ben nodded. He remembered very vividly the image of the young man who'd been forced to go for his gun and how badly he'd been beaten. Ulysses could easily have shamed him but instead, he'd chosen to kill.

The sheriff scratched his jaw. "Mandy isn't going to be too happy with me when I tell her I've decided to hire you as my deputy."

"Why?"

"She's even less impressed by lawmen than she is with hard-rock miners."

"I guess she'd rather marry someone like that young banker fella," Ben said.

"I guess," the sheriff said. "Hell, I don't know. Mandy doesn't tell either me or Mrs. Nye a thing about her beaus. All I know is that she wishes I'd have picked a different line of work. One that payed better, had shorter hours and less danger."

"It's an important job," Ben said. "I got a feeling that I'm going to learn a lot here. How much will I be paid?"

"Fifty cents a day," the sheriff said without batting an eyelash.

"Fifty cents! Why, I won't be able to pay you or Rick back a cent or even help to pay for my groceries at Mrs. Walker's house."

"I guess you'll just have to get a raise pretty damn quick then, won't you?" Nye said. "As soon as you learn how to handle a gun and can lift a two-hundred-pound anvil over your head, then I'll pay you a dollar a day."

"Underground miners get five."

"I know that," the sheriff said with a wink. "But you don't ever want to go underground again, do you."

It wasn't a question. Everyone in Virginia City knew the history of Ben's cowardice in the mine and how it had destroyed George Pope in less than a week.

"No," Ben whispered. "I wouldn't go down in one of those mines for five hundred dollars a day."

"Then take the fifty cents. I've also got you a part-time job down at the emporium loading wagons for old man Yankovich. You'll earn another five dollars a week there in the mornings, but it's the hardest work on the Comstock. If you can stand up to that old man and his slave-driving pace, then you'll sure enough be able to lift a two-hundred-pound anvil overhead in a matter of a few months."

Ben knew Yankovich. The man was a tyrant, but scrupulously fair in all his dealings. "I'm not sure I can stand up to what he'll ask me to do."

"Then let's go have a word with him. I'll tell old Yank that he's going to have to take it easy on you for the first few weeks until you get your strength back. And remember, it's just for the mornings."

"Good thing," Ben said. "Otherwise, he'd kill me for sure."

CHAPTER SEVEN

Ben wiped his brow and finished loading the last of the kegs of nails and supplies that would be used by the Ophir Mine. Sitting close by on the loading dock, the freighter watched with interest, then mopped his brow and said, "Didn't we have one of them flywheels, sent over from San Francisco, included on this shipment?"

Ben checked and rechecked the invoice. Old Yankovich had ordered one all right and it had been paid for in advance. "Let me look around the storeroom," he said.

It was July and the loading dock faced right into the morning sun. Ben had removed his shirt and his powerful torso rippled with muscle as he stepped into the dim storeroom and searched the aisles until he found the flywheel. It was about four feet in diameter and three inches thick, but he picked it up easily and carried it back out to the dock where he placed it on top of the other supplies.

"It's not going to go anywhere," he promised.

The freighter shook his head with admiration. "You're stronger than a damned ox! Maybe you ought to be in the double-drillin' contest and win this year's thousand-dollar prize."

"Not likely I'd enter a miner's contest, even if I thought I could win. Wouldn't be right because I'll never be a miner."

"I heard about your past and about your father, too.

Mighty sad story that. Still, there ought to be some way you could turn all your muscle into some greenback dollars."

The freighter thought a moment, then snapped his fingers. "Say, Ben! You ever think about bare knuckles fighting? Them professional fighters come through here every couple months offering big prize money for anyone that can last three rounds."

Ben's interest was piqued. "I've heard about them. How much can a fella make if he lasts?"

"Couple hundred dollars. And if he should win . . . well, he could make a thousand. Even more if he betted on himself."

"It's an idea," Ben said. "I've never fought anyone in a ring, but I guess I could do a little shadowboxing and give it a try."

"Big and powerful as you are," the freighter said, "all you'd have to do is land one solid punch and you'd win. Hell, no use wasting all that muscle on what that stingy old Yank must be paying you. A young fella like yourself has to start looking out for himself sooner or later."

After the freighter drove away, Ben swept the loading dock, and when the fly-specked clock on the wall said it was noon, old Yank came out to make sure he didn't leave a minute early.

Yank squinted up at the sun, then said, "See you tomorrow at seven."

"Yank, you ever do any fighting?"

The old man blinked. Nearing eighty, he was a little stooped, but still very strong and active. "I fight with my wife every night."

"That's not what I meant," Ben said, raising his fists and

taking a classic fighting stance. "I meant fighting with your fists—in a fighting ring."

Yank stared at the tall, powerful young man who was now dancing playfully around on his loading dock. "Na!" he snorted. "That is a good way to get your brains scrambled. Fighting is a bad thing."

"It pays well, though," Ben said, then winked and added, "given the poor wages I make here and at the sheriff's office, I could use some extra money."

"You'd get your brains scrambled," Yank said, unimpressed by Ben's muscular physique or his fancy footwork.

But by the time Ben had washed the sweat and dirt from his upper body and then tugged on his shirt, the idea of fighting for prize money had fixed very firmly in his mind. That afternoon, he asked Sheriff Nye about it and was surprised when the sheriff said, "It's a fair idea. 'Course, if you lost bad, it could backfire."

"What do you mean?"

Nye propped his boots up on his desk and leaned back in his swivel chair. "Well, since you quit drinking last year, you've gotten so strong that you scare most men into behaving themselves. But if you was to get your butt kicked, then you'd lose face and every drunk in town would want to challenge you to fight."

"I hadn't thought of that." Ben frowned. "Like I told old Yank, I never been in a hard fight. Once in a while, I sorta shove 'em a little when there's trouble. And you know I've had to pistol-whip a couple that were just plain mean."

"Sometimes a lawman has to crack a skull or two to get respect," Nye said. "But understand that the men that come through towns with promoters and their own ring are professionals. Most are as big and strong as you and likely to be more than your match, given their experience. They know how to hit and where to hit. They know all the tricks."

"I never expected I could whip 'em," Ben said. "But if I could stay in the ring long enough to win a couple of hundred dollars in prize money, now that would be something pretty special. I don't suppose, along with the drawing and shooting lessons, that you'd teach me a few tricks."

"Hell, I'm no fighter!"

"Sure you are, Sheriff! I've heard lots of stories about you whipping bigger men. You must know something."

"I don't fight by any rules," Nye said. "When I fight, it's to win and I don't care how. In the ring, there are rules. You can't kick a man or gouge out his eyes or punch him in the throat. You can't bite or stomp him either."

"Seems fairly straightforward. "Anything else?"

"No."

"Then how about a few lessons? I need some help."

The sheriff dropped his feet to the floor and stood up. He was about five-ten and one-fifty, but he was quick and solid. "All right, take a swing at me. A hard one straight for my jaw."

"Now wait . . ."

"Go ahead!"

Ben figured that the sheriff knew what he was doing, so he cocked back his fist and uncorked a straight right. At the same instant, Nye ducked and pounded him in the solar plexis with a hard uppercut.

"Damn, that hurt!" Ben gasped, holding the place just under where his ribs came together.

"Of course it did and I pulled up on the punch," Nye said.

"Next to a man's crotch or this throat, go for the solar plexis. A professional fighter will be taking target practice on it and you'd better learn to protect it if you plan to last more than a minute."

The sheriff stood Ben up and showed him the correct fighting stance. "Keep your elbows in close. Extend the left and use it to jab or feint blows. Then come across with your right. Don't loop your punches but drive them straight off your chest."

Nye demonstrated. "And it doesn't hurt to move a little, rock your head back and forth, keep your chin down and don't close your eyes when you swing."

"There's a lot more to it than I figured," Ben said. "Maybe I was a fool even to think about getting into the ring with a professional fighter. I would probably get myself killed."

"Not likely. If they beat the hell out of the local heroes, they'd be out of opponents real fast and probably wind up in prison. But what they like to do is to take a big strong fella like yourself, who doesn't have anything but heart and brawn, and make a good, bloody show. Their man will take some punches, maybe even pretend he's hurt and then, when the local kid thinks he's got it won and gets just a little careless, wham! He's off to sleep."

Ben listened carefully. His solar plexis still hurt and it left him with a weak, hollow feeling inside. He had no doubt that, had the sheriff wanted to, he could have left him writhing on the floor.

The sheriff gave him a few more pointers and then asked him to practice his stance and his punches. "Shadowboxing is good for you. Keep moving and punching. Don't punch hard, but try to punch fast. You've already got more than enough natural strength to stand toe to toe with anyone. It's quickness that you have to worry about."

"Same as with a gun, huh?"

"That's right. But I've taught you that there's always some way to compensate for your disadvantages. With a gun, it's coolness under fire and deadly accuracy."

"And with my fists?"

"It's your power," Nye said simply. "I have no doubt whatsoever that you could knock out—with one blow—anyone that ever steps in front of you."

Ben smiled. "How soon can I be ready to have a chance at this?"

"Let's give it a month before we start thinking about you entering a contest," Nye said. "And if you're smart, you'll tell nobody. Especially my daughter."

"I expect that she won't be too pleased at the idea."

"She'll be madder than hell," the sheriff said. "At both of us."

Ben did not reveal that he intended to use his winnings to buy Mandy an engagement ring. He figured she'd laugh outright at his proposal of marriage, but a man had to have a diamond ring just in case she said yes.

During the weeks that followed, it wasn't easy not to tell Mandy about his plan to win some prize money, but Ben kept his mouth shut and trained hard. He saw fights, or rather brawls, almost daily in Virginia City. Not once, however, did he observe what he would call a real pugilist or someone that had taken a little time to learn how to deliver a correct blow. And now, with the sheriff tutoring him daily, he watched the fights with a very critical eye. He noted how most men came in swinging from every direction, looking to finish the fight with one punch. And usually, the first man who landed a clean blow did end the contest. There was never any attempt at defensive maneuvering or at blocking punches. No one ducked or moved their heads to make them a more difficult target—except one afternoon when Ben saw a little Englishman take on two much bigger men.

It was obvious that the scrappy Englishman had learned the science of proper boxing. He combined speed, excellent footwork and wonderful defensive skills to keep his two larger opponents at bay. His hands were a blur, and when they struck flesh, they left a mark. He was not a heavy puncher, but he was elusive and actually winning the fight until he tripped over an outstretched leg. Once down, it was clear he would be stomped to pieces, so Ben drew his sixgun and fired two shots into the air.

"That's enough!"

The two men looked as if they'd been beaten by a mob. Their noses were bloodied and their eyes were swelling shut. "You've had your fun," Ben said, unable to hide his amusement. "Now go along."

"We didn't have any fun at all!" one of the men shouted. "Deputy, you saw who was getting in all the good licks before he went down. Now it's our turn!"

"Uh-uh," Ben said, leveling his gun.

The men beat a hasty retreat and Ben helped the Englishman to his feet. In gratitude, the fighter bought Ben a glass of sarsaparilla in the Bucket of Blood Saloon while he enjoyed his dark ale.

Ben studied the man closely. He looked almost bookwormish and anything but a pugilist. "Where did you learn to fight like that?"

"In London when I was much younger than you are," the Englishman said, introducing himself as Wiley Prickett. "I was once a professional, you know. And I still like to keep my hand in it. If God had granted me your size and obvious strength, I'd have been champion of the whole bloody universe."

"You did pretty well, being just the size you are now," Ben told him.

"Thanks. But you really did save my bones, Deputy. I wish there was something I could do to repay you, but unfortunately, I'm a little low on funds right at the moment; you understand."

"Sure, but if you mean it, you could repay me with a boxing lesson," Ben said.

Prickett grinned. "The only lessons I give are with my fists. That's how I learned and that's the only way I know how to teach."

"I'm willing to take a few punches to learn."

Prickett quaffed down his ale and said, "I believe this door leads to the back alley. Shall we?"

They stood apart, and Prickett raised his hands and Ben did the same. The Englishman smiled. "Good! At least you know the correct boxing stance. Now, anytime you are ready, attack me."

Ben remembered the blow to his solar plexis and pulled his elbows in close to protect himself. He began to sway back and forth, and as he came forward, he tried to remember to stay loose and quick.

Prickett feinted a left and Ben stayed to home, avoiding a
sure right cross to his face.

"Excellent!" Prickett cried. "Ninety-nine men out of a
hundred would have gone for that nice feint."

"Thank you," Ben said, feinting his own left and then driving a right that narrowly missed the man's jaw. For his failure,
he took a hard blow to the ribs that caused him to grunt with
pain. Prickett, it seemed, was not holding back anything.

"I've broken ribs lighter than your own with that punch,"
the Englishman said, his eyes sparking with excitement. It was
clear to Ben that the man was having a wonderful time and
probably setting him up for a slaughter.

Prickett again feinted a left, then a right and then another
left, which all happened so fast that Ben was caught off guard
and earned a hard punch to the point of his jaw that actually
drove him back a half step.

"You have a jaw of rock," the Englishman said, momen-
tarily rubbing his bruised knuckles.

Ben circled warily. So far, despite all his practice and the
best fighting advice that Sheriff Nye could give him, he still
had not landed a single punch. And if . . .

Prickett swarmed in on him. Suddenly, Ben felt his face
being tattooed by the smaller man's bony fists. He tasted
blood, struck out blindly and missed again and again. He
could hear Prickett grunting each time his own fists scored
solidly. Ben was already angry. He was getting cut to pieces
and hadn't gotten in one good blow yet.

Ben felt himself stagger back. His face was numb and
Prickett was smiling, looking very happy and maddeningly
unsullied. "Have you had enough yet? Should I slow down
and explain?"

"Yeah," Ben said. "Slow down and explain."

Prickett's fist snapped out to pop Ben in the nose. A trickle of blood seeped down his upper lip. "I don't think that would be wise."

Ben blinked, realizing that he had stopped bobbing his head and was as motionless as a big punching bag. He began to move again, back and forth, then in a circle to his left. Prickett was now stalking him like a hungry cat.

Two more stiff lefts snapped his head back as Prickett moved in, swarming all over him with punches until Ben drove a powerful uppercut from somewhere down close to his knees. The blow caught Prickett in the belly and lifted him a foot off the ground. The Englishman's face went chalk-white and his cheeks puffed out.

Ben hammered him with a left cross the moment Prickett's feet hit the ground. When the Englishman hit the dirt, he skidded another two feet and lay still.

Ben rushed to Prickett's side and pulled the Englishman up into a sitting position. "Are you all right!"

Prickett *wasn't* all right. He was knocked out cold. Ben picked the man up and rushed through the alley to C Street. He dropped the Englishman in the nearest horse watering trough. Prickett sank, then came up spluttering and swinging.

"Take it easy!" Ben said. "The fight is over."

Prickett's eyes began to focus. He looked at Ben quite strangely and said, "I think you hit me with a lucky punch, but I'm afraid to test that theory, so why don't we shake hands and let it go at that?"

"Suits me right down to the ground," Ben said. He started to offer Prickett his hand and then thought better of it. He liked the Englishman, but he didn't trust him. "I'd better check in with the sheriff right now, so I'll see you around."

It was almost a month before a fighter came to town. The man was named "Masher" Mongolis and he stood at least six foot six inches tall and outweighed Ben by more than forty pounds. The fight was staged at Piper's Opera House and the place was filled to capacity.

"Gentlemen!" the promoter cried, parading around the ring while Masher glared with hatred at the drunks who taunted him from a safe distance. "What we are about to have is a contest of courage and strength. Those stout-hearted among you can—for only ten dollars—win the opportunity to defeat Masher Mongolis or even to co-exist with him in this ring for three rounds. Should you prevail, you will win five hundred dollars for a victory! And if you just manage to survive three rounds, you can win one hundred dollars."

"How fast can that big bastard run!" a drunk shouted.

"Faster than you can," one of his friends yelled as the crowd exploded with laughter.

The promoter allowed the audience to banter for several minutes. It was a show and it was fun. But it wasn't making him any money, and when he called for volunteers, no one wanted to be first. Now Masher Mongolis began to incite the crowd with taunts.

"You're a bunch of cowards!" he bellowed at them. "A bunch of sissies! I heard there were *men* on the Comstock, but I heard wrong. You people oughta wear dresses!"

The hard-rock miners were stung deeply. Their pride had been injured, their manhood disparaged. "I'll whip your big ass!" a big miner shouted, and the room began to fill with cheers.

Ben found he was cheering as well, even though on one side of him, Prickett was very quiet, and on the other, Sheriff Nye stood with his arms folded across his chest.

The sheriff said, "They're playing this crowd like an out-of-tune piano."

Prickett agreed. "But Masher will give this fool the better part of three rounds. He'll pretend to be hurt and then, with about one minute remaining, when the crowd is cheering its heart out, he'll take his head off with a single blow."

Ben watched the fight progress exactly as Prickett had predicted. The miner was strong and he was brave. Each time he landed a punch on the Masher, the crowd went crazy. And by the third round, the crowd was yelling itself hoarse. Masher was against the ropes and acting like he was about to fall when, suddenly, he bent over and drove a vicious uppercut to the miner's solar plexis.

The miner's face turned the same sickly white as a fish's belly. His mouth made an "O" and Masher filled it with his knuckles. The miner's eyes rolled up in his head and he crashed to the canvas.

The crowd's cheer died and men stood with open-mouthed amazement as their hero lay quivering.

Nye nodded and looked at Ben. "Solar plexis punch, like I told you. Bloodless, so as not to scare away any other fools."

The promoter gonged his bell to signal the end of the round and the fight. The prostrated miner had his knees drawn up to his chin in a fetal position and his groans could be heard throughout the great hall.

"Well, Ben," the sheriff said. "You want a try at the Masher?"

Ben did not, but he'd made the mistake of telling a few men in town about his ambitious plan and now his name was heard. "Ben Pope! Bring on Ben Pope!"

Ben sighed. He was trapped and he was afraid he was going to be hurt and humiliated. He looked at Prickett. "I thought you might want to go first."

"No thanks. I'm going to sit the evening out. The Masher is a bit too much for a skinny chap like me. But I'd say he's just your size."

Prickett grinned. "Actually, I've fought him before."

Ben waited with growing impatience as the sound of his name echoed loudly in the great opera hall. Finally, Ben shouted, "And what happened to you!"

Prickett shrugged. "Actually, I thought I had him until he drove his forehead into my nose and broke it all to bloody hell. He'll do that if it's close. You should try and remember that if you can."

"Thanks a lot," Ben said. He turned to Sheriff Nye. "You have any more helpful advice?"

"Short of taking your gun in the ring, I'd say the best thing you can do is claim an immediate case of severe indigestion. Fighting him isn't worth a hundred dollars. I've seen a lot easier men offering the same prize money. My advice would be to pass on this mean bastard."

Ben would have taken that advice, but now the crowd was roaring his name and people were shoving and prodding him forward. He *was* trapped!

When he climbed into the ring, his heart was beating so

fast he was sure he was going to seize up and die, even before Masher Mongolis had a chance to rearrange his face.

"Well, look at this fine specimen of manhood!" the promoter shouted to a now silent and very hopeful crowd. "This young fella looks like he could whip grizzly bears! Are there any bettors in this lively crowd?"

A ground swell of affirmation flowed over the ring from every corner of the hall. "Good!" the promoter cried. "I'll offer five-to-one odds that Masher Mongolis will stop this fine lad in less than the required three rounds. Are there any takers!"

"Damn right!" someone shouted as he raised a fistful of money. "I got fifty dollars says that our Virginia City deputy can last!"

Ben shook his head. "Now wait a minute," he protested loudly. "It's one thing to get my face bashed in, but it's *my* face. I can't let you men risk your money on me!"

"Why the hell not!" another miner shouted. "The odds are better than at the gambling tables!"

Before Ben could say anything more, a great many bets were being taken by men employed by the promoter and scattered throughout the crowd for this very purpose. The promoter walked over to Ben and said, "You ever been in a ring before?"

"No." Ben gave him the ten dollars he'd saved. "But I'll take those five-to-one odds and bet on myself."

"Good! I like men with confidence. Now, the rules are the same as I explained earlier. No kicking, biting, gouging, or feet or fists to the crotch or the throat. When you fall, I'll make sure that Masher doesn't get carried away and stomp you."

"Thanks."

"You're welcome. Just try to put on a good show for your friends. If it gets rough, don't run! That discourages anyone else from fighting. Just scream or in some other way let me know you're hurtin' bad and I'll tell Masher to ease up. Understand me?"

"I think so," Ben said, knowing the promoter was doing a job with his head. Ben gazed across the ring and waved at Masher Mongolis, who was glaring and yelling taunts at the fast-betting crowd.

"All right, gentlemen!" the promoter yelled. "Has everyone placed their bets?"

The crowd was ready. The promoter rang his bell and Ben sent a swift little prayer toward heaven. Masher Mongolis beat his bare chest and came lumbering across the ring. Ben wanted to turn and run. The man was huge! He raised his fists and growled like a crazed animal, then he swung and Ben almost forgot to duck.

When Masher's fist slid over his head, Ben was so shocked at the immensity of his opponent that he forgot to swing back and missed an easy opportunity to pound Masher's ribs. Realizing his mistake, Ben jumped forward, then turned and tried to get his feet to move a little. He danced and the crowd cheered wildly.

"Show-off, huh?" Masher hissed. "Well, I like them kind."

Masher feinted three jabs and then sent a thunderbolt left that grazed Ben's jaw and knocked the sense back into him. While the man's left was still extended, Ben came in close and dug two powerful hooks to Masher's body. The giant grunted both times and Ben was encouraged to see a flicker of pain shoot up into the man's eyes.

His encouragement was short-lived, however. Masher caught him with a sneaky overhand that sent him back-pedaling into one of the corner poles. Before Ben could push out and get away, Masher hit him twice in the face and Ben's knees buckled, but he managed to duck and get out of the corner.

The crowd went wild a moment later when Ben unleashed a thundering left, and before Masher could recover, followed it with a sledging right to the side of the jaw that half turned Masher around. Ben realized that, while he might be smaller, he was more powerful and he was quicker. His confidence soared and he lunged at his hurt opponent, but the bell sounded.

Prickett, Nye and even Rick Kilbane was in his corner and all of them were offering advice at the same time.

"You hurt him with those punches to the gut," Sheriff Nye was saying. "Keep pounding him in the body!"

But Wiley Prickett was yelling, "He's open for a left hook to the chin, throw it!"

And Rick added, "You stupid sonofabitch, now he's mad and the best thing you can do is take my gun and shoot him!"

Ben kept nodding his head and watching Masher, who, if anything, looked more determined.

The bell sounded again and the Masher practically threw himself across the ring. Ben wasn't quite ready and Masher caught him with his hands down. Two brutal punches sent him skidding across the ring. His vision blurred and his brain seemed to go to sleep for a moment, and when he looked up, he saw the promoter counting to eight. Ben jumped to his feet and raised his hands to cover his head. Masher took full advantage and started hooking him to the gut and the ribs.

"Grab him!" Prickett shouted. "Grab him!"

Ben grabbed the bigger man and hugged him for all he was worth. He locked his hand on his wrist and tried to break Masher's ribs. In return, Masher began to butt him with his forehead. Ben was stunned again and went reeling back as the crowd shouted and booed.

Masher thought he had his man and left himself open for a minute. With all of his strength, Ben stepped forward instead of retreating as expected and he buried his fist in Masher's solar plexis. Masher bellowed in agony. His arms fell at his side and Ben was on him swinging from all angles as the house went insane.

Masher was going down. Ben kept hitting him. The giant's eyes were glazed and his legs were rubbery. Suddenly, the bell sounded and the promoter was screaming for Ben to step back and go to his corner.

"You've got him!" Rick shouted. "You're going to whip him!"

But Prickett was less optimistic. "Just don't get overconfident," he yelled loud enough to be heard over the crowd. "And watch his forehead. If you turn your face up to him, he'll break your nose too."

"You're doing great, Deputy," Nye said. "You plant one more boomer in his solar plexis and he's out on the floor. Just one more punch like that and it's over."

Ben nodded. He could hear the crowd chanting his name. Across the ring, Masher wasn't glaring anymore, he looked confused and worried.

The bell sounded, and this time, it was Ben who was across the ring first. He feinted a left, then a right and then he pounded Masher in the face with a short left cross that sent the bigger man staggering and the crowd to its feet. Ben was on the fighter, knowing that Masher would have done the same to him. He had an open shot at Masher's nose, but instead smashed his jaw and sent him backpedaling against the ropes.

"Finish him!" Rick shrieked.

"Solar plexis!" the sheriff screamed.

"Left hook to the jaw again!" Prickett bellowed, pounding on the ring's apron and yelling himself hoarse.

Ben threw himself at Masher and drove two more punches to the fighter's face, then actually lifted the man up on his toes with a mighty punch to his belly. Masher Mongolis, with an expression of disbelief, tried to grab Ben as he toppled forward and struck the canvas.

The bell was ringing and the promoter was trying to get his fighter to his corner, but the fight was over as the crowd swarmed over and under the ropes. The chanting grew louder and louder, and Ben, bloody and covered with sweat, was hoisted up while men cheered and threw their hats in the air.

He had won! He had erased the label of coward that had haunted him since that day in the Lucky Eagle Mine. Ben raised his battered fist and bellowed in triumph. "This one's for George Pope! This one's for my father!"

CHAPTER EIGHT

"Deal me out," Rick said, tossing his cards on the poker table and standing up.

Ulysses Kilbane slammed his fist down so hard that the drinks jumped and spilled. "What the hell is wrong with you!" he demanded. "We can carry the loss. Sit back down!"

Rick felt every eye in the room turn to him. He had been playing high-stakes poker for nearly six hours and his luck had run as cold as a Sierra stream. "Another day," he said. "My luck isn't going to change and I'll try it again tomorrow."

Ulysses' beefy face colored red and he took another big draft of whiskey. "I told you to sit back down!"

"No." Rick turned his back on the table and walked across the saloon to a table near the front where Jenny French waited anxiously for him. "Mind if I join you for a drink?"

"Sit down," Jenny said quietly, "but face Ulysses. Please!"

Rick's smile was frozen on his lips. He chose a seat with his back toward his father and raised his hand for a bottle. Rick had never before openly defied his father and it had taken every bit of courage he could muster, as evidenced by the fact that his hands were shaking. "What's the matter," he said. "You think he's going to shoot his own son?"

"He looks mad enough," Jenny said. "I don't think you should have turned your back on him and walked away like that. You know his murderous rages."

"I'm his only son," Rick said. "What's he doing now?"

"Shuffling the deck."

Jenny leaned close so that she could not possibly be over-heard, though there was no one even close to them. The building tension had driven the wiser, more sober customers to other bars. Jenny asked, "Has he started using the holdout again?"

Rick nodded. His father was using a device that strapped onto his arm and had a tension spring that could feed him cards directed by the motion of his foot. It was a revolutionary cheating device that almost no one on the Comstock had heard about yet. And by the time they did learn of its exis-tence, Ulysses would be happy to discard the cheating device while he was tens of thousands of dollars richer.

Rick poured himself a stiff drink. "He's up against a pair of gunfighters that won't back down from him if they even sus-pect he's cheating. I wish he'd just take his losses or walk away from the game."

"How much has he dropped?"

"About three thousand. I dropped nearly sixteen hundred. Pa will never stand for that. He'll pull guns on 'em if they try to walk out with that much of the house's money. That's why I came over here and that's why you've got to go upstairs before lead starts flying."

"He'll get himself killed!" Jenny hissed. "And he'll deserve it, but I won't let him have you killed too."

"If he's in trouble," Rick said, "I'm going to help him anyway I can. There's just nothing else that I can do."

"Don't be a fool, Rick!"

In answer, he smiled and drank again. "It's a matter of

honor," he said. "My honor, my decision. Now, before there's trouble, I want you to clear on out of here."

Jenny French nodded. "Will you come up to the room as soon as this is over?"

"Sure."

Realizing that she had little choice but to go, Jenny stood up and kissed him on the lips, then hurried toward the stairs. Rick watched her climb the stairs and he could see the curve of her leg. Jenny had a bounce to her and he liked the way her hips swayed when she moved. Watching Jenny was one of his favorite pastimes and he did not take his eyes off her until she disappeared from sight.

Rick finished his drink and moved around so that his back was against the wall. When an acquaintance started to bring his beer over, Rick shook his head almost imperceptibly and the message was clear enough to send the man back to the bar. He left the beer and hurried quickly outside.

An hour passed very slowly. Rick drank little and his tension mounted because Ulysses, even with the holdout, was having trouble winning. The holdout was not foolproof and a man didn't use it on every hand he was dealt. He'd use it as little as possible and then only when the stakes were high enough to justify the risk.

From across the room, Rick could see his father's foot moving constantly, which meant that, in his anger and frustration, Ulysses had thrown caution aside and was using the mechanical device with reckless frequency. Rick figured it was just a matter of time before the device was discovered and the fireworks would begin.

Other men in the room must have figured the same because, when they finished their drinks, they headed for the door where a large crowd had collected to gawk and whisper. Everyone expected a fight; they'd seen all the signs of one brewing in the Silver Dollar for many hours. They knew Ulysses would never stand to lose big money.

It was almost evening when the pile of chips bet on one hand escalated to over seven hundred dollars. The saloon was still empty and Rick had not moved in three hours or touched his whiskey since Jenny French had gone upstairs to wait for him.

"Two pair!" one of the winning gunfighters said.

"Three deuces," the other growled with a smug, confident expression on his face.

The old gambler studied his cards for a long minute and then he laid them face up. "Three tens," he said. "You boys finally lose."

Ulysses reached forward with his left hand for the pile of chips, but one of the gunfighters came to his feet with a gun in his hand and said, "Take off that coat and roll up your right sleeve, Ulysses. I want to make sure you ain't got something hidden in there."

Ulysses studied the gun and then the crowd of spectators. "Are you accusing me of cheating?" he asked in a very loud voice. " 'Cause if you are, you're dead men."

The second stranger pulled his gun. "There's only one way to find out. Stand up, take off that coat and let's see your bare right arm."

Ulysses stood up. He'd been accused of playing with crooked cards all of his life, but no one had ever lived to back up the charge. There was no way in hell he was going to roll up his sleeve, with a mechanical device strapped to his arm, for all of Virginia City to witness.

Ulysses glanced at Rick and the signal was obvious. He needed an edge in this fight and Rick had better be that edge.

"Drop your guns on the table!" Rick said, drawing his side arm and cocking it loudly. "If you turn around, you're dead."

The two men froze, but it took them a long time to finally drop their guns. When they did pitch them on the poker table, one said, "So you're the joker in this setup. Well, I'd been led to believe that you always stayed out of your old man's crooked dealings. Guess I was wrong."

Ulysses cursed. His hand closed around the neck of a whiskey bottle and he smashed the gunfighter across the side of his head. The bottle shattered and the man staggered, his scalp badly cut. He leaned forward to keep from falling and he said in a strangled voice, "You old sonofabitch, I should have killed you an hour ago!"

In reply, Ulysses grabbed the man's gun from the table and shot him in the chest.

"Pa!" Rick cried. "What . . ."

Ulysses turned his gun on the second man. "Say good-bye to this world," he grated.

"No! Please, at least give me a fighting chance!"

But Ulysses gunned him down. The gunfighter's arms blew out from his sides and then the impact of three bullets knocked him backward over his chair.

Ulysses scooped up everyone's winnings and dumped them into one of the gunfighters' Stetson. He was grinning when he looked at Rick and then at the bartender and spectators outside. "It was self-defense, wasn't it?"

The men crowded around the bat-wing doors nodded, but Rick just looked away. He'd known that his father was brutal and would kill without remorse, but he'd never seen him shoot men down in cold blood before and then smile. Ulysses actually seemed happy and that shocked the hell out of Rick.

"All right, everyone!" Ulysses called. "Drinks on the house!"

Rick happened to glance up and see Jenny at the top of the stairs. Even at a distance, he could see the worry in her eyes, but he turned away and strolled to the bar. He had defied his father once this day. He would not now humiliate him by refusing to drink at his side.

Ulysses was flushed with excitement and whiskey. He clapped Rick on the back and laughed. "We make a hell of a pair, don't we!"

"Yeah," Rick said without enthusiasm. "But why'd you have to kill them? Couldn't you have just . . ."

Ulysses grabbed him by the arm and jerked him toward the back of the room away from the others.

Rick threw off his father's grip. "What really bothers me, Pa, is that you *like* killing, don't you!"

"They were gunfighters and they were cheating me!" Ulysses hissed. "It was them or us, dammit. Can't you understand that?"

Rick shook his head. "I never saw them cheating. And if they were, we should have run them out of our saloon."

"And what about all their winnin's? We gonna let them take that too! Use your head!"

"I don't want to be a part of murder again," Rick said, glancing at the two dead men. "I've killed—you know I'm no coward—but I don't ever want to do something like this again."

Ulysses' face twisted with boiling rage. "You're my son and my partner. I expect you to stand with me all the way. And if the chips are down, you'd better be on my side, no matter what. Is that clear?"

"Yeah," Rick said, finally looking away with his mouth dry and his chest feeling tight. "It couldn't be clearer."

"Good," Ulysses said, his mood swinging completely around and his anger vanishing. "Let's have a few drinks and put this behind us."

Rick went behind the bar and took a full bottle. He was not a big drinker, but this night, he intended to get drunk. Taking the bottle, he walked to an empty table and sat down with his back to the room. Nobody dared approach him.

He drank hard and fast for nearly an hour before Sheriff Nye shoved his way into the saloon and pronounced, "Ulysses Kilbane, you're under arrest."

"What for!" Ulysses bellowed drunkenly.

Nye pointed to the two dead gunfighters that no one had even bothered to move. "For murder. Raise your arms, then take off your coat slow and easy. I want to see what you've got up your sleeve."

Rick swallowed. His father had forgotten to get rid of the holdout! Now, he was trapped. The holdout was all the evidence that the sheriff would need to have Ulysses Kilbane tried for cheating and murder.

Ulysses also realized his blunder, but there was nothing that he could do except obey the order. He slowly pulled off his coat, his eyes darting from Rick to his bartender and then to the sheriff, who stood with his gun leveled.

"Try it," Nye murmured, almost pleading. "Just try and pull a derringer or a knife. Nothing would please me more than to save the good citizens of this city the waste of their tax dollars. Come on. Be brave! Try it!"

Ulysses was desperate to try something. But Nye was deadly, so Ulysses shrugged out of his coat.

"Now roll up your sleeve, Kilbane. And let's see what kind of surprise we have waiting for all of us."

Ulysses shook his head in dogged refusal. He licked his lips and his eyes touched Rick's with a silent plea, but Rick didn't move—he'd be damned if he'd kill the sheriff, and nothing less than killing would do under these circumstances.

Ulysses swung his eyes to the bartender and then he smiled and looked back at the sheriff. "*You* roll up my sleeves, Sheriff. I don't feel like doing it myself."

The bartender was slowly reaching for the shotgun that he kept hidden behind the bar. Half drunk, Rick watched as the bartender raised the shotgun and started to level it at the sheriff even as Nye caught the movement out of the corner of his eye. The lawman swung around and fired all in one motion and the bartender took a bullet in the forehead causing the shotgun to discharge both barrels upward into a huge crystal chandelier which disintegrated into a million pieces. As the glass showered down on Nye, the lawman instinctively raised his hands in an attempt to shield his eyes.

The momentary diversion was all the edge that Ulysses needed, even if he was drunk. Ulysses' sixgun filled his big hand and emptied itself into the sheriff's body. Rick stiffened as four bullets sent Nye goose-stepping backward. The man's face was a mixture of sadness and anger, and even as he was taking the bullets, he was trying to bring his own gun to bear on Ulysses. Somehow he got one shot off, but it went wild and buried itself high in the wall.

Sheriff Nye was dead before he struck the floor.

For a long moment, there wasn't a sound, just the smoke

and the smell of gunpowder. Then, Ulysses shook his head as if in a daze and a wide smile creased his face. Without a word, he grabbed a bottle and headed upstairs to the women.

Rick could not take his eyes off the dead sheriff until Jenny French screamed in fear, "Let go of me!"

Rick saw his father wrestling at the top of the stairs with Jenny. He leaped out of his chair and ran to the stairs. His gun was in his fist and he did not even remember drawing it when he aimed up the staircase at his father and said, "Let go of her or I'll kill you, Pa."

Ulysses hesitated a moment, then he hurled Jenny away from him as if she were a piece of trash. She struck the wall and then came tumbling down the stairs. Rick caught her, but not before she was almost at the bottom.

"Jenny!"

She was unconscious and her right arm was twisted at an unnatural angle. Rick scooped her up in his arms and raced outside to find a doctor. And as the men parted, he could hear Ulysses roaring with fury and triumph as he slammed open the doors hunting his women.

CHAPTER NINE

Ben Pope was down in nearby Gold Hill investigating the background of a crooked machinery salesman who had bilked one of the local mines when he received the tragic news of the shoot-out in the Silver Dollar Saloon.

The rider who notified him of Sheriff Nye's death was named Abe Dawson. Abe had once aspired to be a lawman but could never get hired or elected, so he tended to compensate by cozying up to the local sheriff or magistrate and sometimes even provided helpful information. Because of this, he had been tolerated by Sheriff Nye, despite the fact that he was nettlesome and gossipy.

"It was murder!" Abe said, his voice shaking with righteous anger. "I was peeking under the bat-wing doors when I saw it all happen. First Ulysses guns down the pair he was losin' money to at poker, then the sheriff came and got the drop on him."

Abe shook his head. "But Ulysses, he's smart. He waited until the bartender pulled his shotgun, and when the sheriff turned, Ulysses saw his opening. Yes sir! Faster than a snake kin strike, he drew and shot Mr. Nye four times in the chest! It was terrible!"

"I can't believe he's dead," Ben whispered. "It doesn't seem possible. The sheriff distrusted Ulysses so much that he would have been prepared for any kind of trick."

"Nye was one of the best, but he was no match for Ulysses Kilbane," Abe said. "I guess he was pretty good to you, huh, Deputy?"

Ben cleared his throat. "I owe him . . . well, he's the one that gave me back some pride. Taught me how to fight to win, but never to hurt anyone unless there was no choice."

"What are you goin' to do about Ulysses? You try to arrest him, he'll kill you like he did the sheriff. You ain't near his match, Deputy."

"We'll see," Ben said in a voice that shook with anger. "We'll just see." Reaching up, he dragged Abe from his lathered old horse and dragged him right out of the saddle.

"What the hell are you doin'!" Abe squawked.

"I'm borrowing your horse," Ben said, swinging into the saddle without bothering to lengthen the stirrups. His knees were bent uncomfortably, but he did not care as he whipped the man's skinny old horse into a trot.

"Sheriff, if you kill him, you owe me twenty dollars!"

"I'm not the sheriff!" he yelled over his shoulder. There was a steep divide that separated Gold Hill from Virginia City, and as he neared the top, the horse began to stagger under the unaccustomed heavy rider and fast pace. Not having twenty dollars to spare, Ben piled off the animal and scrambled over the divide and into Virginia City on foot.

Ben's immediate impulse had been to go directly to the Silver Dollar Saloon and arrest Ulysses. However, by the time he reached the sheriff's office, he knew that he had better hold up and use his head. And to be honest, he was scared. If Sheriff Nye, with all his skill and knowledge, had been outfoxed and shot down by Ulysses, then Ben knew he stood little chance of making an arrest.

"Ben!" Mandy cried, throwing herself into his arms when he entered the sheriff's office. "You heard!"

"Just now," he said, holding her gently. "I'm sorry."

Mandy looked up at him. Her eyes were red from crying, but they burned with outrage. "Ulysses may have killed my father, but it was Rick and the bartender that set him up."

Ben shook his head. "Not Rick. I heard about it and Rick played no part in the shooting."

"But he did!" Mandy cried. "He helped Ulysses kill the first two men! And when my father came into that saloon, he knew what Rick had done and that he had to be watched. It cost him his life!"

Ben gently pushed her away, just as he tried to push her words from his mind. Mandy was wrong. She was upset. She didn't know what she was saying. "That's not true."

"But it *is* true!" Mandy reached up and turned his face to her. "I know he's your best friend, but . . ."

"Listen," Ben said, interrupting Mandy before she could say any more. "I better go make arrangements for your father to be taken to the funeral parlor. Go home and comfort your mother."

"No!" Mandy cried. "I want Ulysses and Rick Kilbane arrested for murder!"

"Not Rick," Ben told her in a hard voice. "Ulysses is the one that's going to hang for murder."

Mandy stared at Ben as though she were seeing him for the very first time. "How can you be so blind!" she whispered. "I told you a long time ago that Rick was just like his father. He's a killer! He's as responsible for my father's death as Ulysses. He killed Father just as surely as if he'd pulled the trigger."

Ben knew there was no sense in trying to argue with Mandy. She was devastated by her father's death and she wasn't thinking clearly. If she had been, she'd have realized that there wasn't a jury in the country that would say Rick was guilty of murder.

He tried to be patient. "Listen," he began. "I know how you feel. Your father was like a father to me as well. But that doesn't change the fact that no judge or jury would find Rick responsible for his death. I can't . . . and I won't arrest Rick Kilbane."

Mandy seemed to grow calm. She turned and looked out the window a moment, and when she spoke, her voice was very soft. "I had a dream about you, Ben. I never told you because it was a nightmare. I saw no reason to alarm you and I always thought you'd go to California and become a farmer as you wanted."

Ben selected a shotgun from the rifle rack. He broke it and made sure that it was loaded, though he knew it would be. Closing the breech with a hard snap, he said, "Mandy, I got no time to listen to stories. Ulysses will be waiting for me and I got to start thinking about getting him in this jail without being killed."

Mandy went on as if she hadn't heard him speak. "I dreamed that you were gunned down. That's what I never told you. And it wasn't Ulysses that pulled the trigger, it was Rick."

Ben shuddered inside, then he grabbed the door handle saying, "If you got any special prayers, say one for me right now. The minute I step into the Silver Dollar, I'll be needing all the help I can get."

The sun was sliding behind Sun Mountain when Ben

crossed C Street. His deputy star was polished, as were his boots. He wore a black Stetson hat and a nice calfskin vest. His stride was long and betrayed none of the fear that roiled inside of him as he headed for the Silver Dollar Saloon.

There was a crowd waiting near the saloon and some of its members spoke to him, but Ben paid them no attention because his mind was locked on the seemingly impossible task of getting Ulysses into his jail. Ben did not even consider what he would do if Rick tried to interfere. Rick, his blood brother, the one he'd sworn always to be loyal to, no matter what kind of trouble might come between them.

A hush fell over the crowd at the Silver Dollar Saloon when Ben stepped inside. The shotgun was cradled across the bend in his thick right arm and he paused, remembering how Sheriff Nye had always warned him to allow his eyes a few moments to adjust to the dimness of a saloon after coming out of bright sunshine.

Ben saw where the saloon floor had just been scrubbed of its fresh blood. The flooring was still wet and they hadn't done a very good job mopping up because he could see a red stain. It made Ben want to pull his gun and kill Ulysses on sight.

"Ben," Rick called in a tired voice. "I'm over here."

Ben turned quickly to see Rick and Jenny sitting together. "It's not you I want. It's Ulysses. Where is he?"

"Put the shotgun down before you make things any worse than they already are," Rick said, his voice weary and sad.

"Where is he?" Ben repeated, as he peered into every corner of the saloon.

"Upstairs. Drunk and whorin'."

Ben headed for the stairs, but Rick's voice stopped him

cold. "My friend, if you barge up there without me, someone is going to die. Most likely it'll be you, but it could also be one of the women. I don't think you want that to happen."

"No," Ben said, turning around and walking back to Rick's table, "I don't."

"Bartender!" Rick said loudly enough to make Ben realize his old friend was a little drunk, especially when Rick snapped his fingers and added, "Oh, I forgot, your friend Nye shot and killed our bartender. Guess I'll get us drinks myself."

Before Ben could say anything, Rick was on his feet and moving toward the bar. "You drink nothing but milk, water or sarsaparilla. Right, old buddy?"

"That's right."

Ben turned to Jenny. "Is he a part of this?"

"No," she said. "He tried to stop it, but Ulysses was a crazy man when he began to lose so much money."

Jenny reached out and gripped his arm. "Listen," she said in a rushed voice, "Rick has been drinking hard since the shoot-out. That isn't like him. You know that."

"Sure, but . . ."

Jenny didn't let him finish. "He knew you'd come and that's why he's drinking. He can't stand the thought of trouble coming between the two of you."

"I can't let this be," Ben told her. "Sheriff Nye was like my own father!"

"Rick understands that, which is why he's going to go up and see his father and try to talk him into surrendering into your custody."

"When hell freezes over!" Ben responded in anger. "I know a thing or two about Ulysses Kilbane. He won't go to jail. Not for me anymore than he would have for Sheriff Nye."

"Then Rick is prepared to make the arrest himself," Jenny said. "He figures that he's the only one that can do it. Ulysses would kill you for certain."

Ben forced himself to relax. "That's what everyone keeps telling me. But I'm the one wearing the badge—not Rick. It's *my* job."

Ben started to pull away, but Jenny held his arm. "Please," she said. "Let Rick go up there and try to talk his father into coming down without a fight. And if that fails, then let Rick handle it."

Ben unpried her fingers from his arm. "I can't do that," he said. "Ulysses is a crazy man when he's drunk. He might even shoot Rick. Then how would I feel? Even worse than I do now, if that was possible."

Ben stood up to signal that the discussion was over. "I'm sorry. I can't do it."

Jenny shrugged her pretty shoulders. "Well," she said. "I promised Rick I'd at least try and talk some sense into you. I guess I can't do any more."

"No, you can't," Ben said.

But when he turned away, he saw that Rick was gone. Instead of getting them something to drink, he'd used Jenny's distraction as an excuse to rush upstairs.

Ben hurried across the saloon floor and took the stairs two steps at a time. When he reached the upper landing, he could hear Rick and Ulysses arguing violently. Ben tiptoed down the hall to an open door and flattened against the wall to listen.

"I won't go to no jail!" Ulysses shouted. "Now git outa here and leave me alone!"

"You have to go," Rick said. "I promised myself I'd bring

you down before Ben Pope comes up here with a gun in his fist."

"Let him come!" Ulysses boomed. "I'll kill him too!"

There was a long pause and then Rick said in a defeated voice. "All right. I'll send him up. But you better get some pants on and get that woman out of the room."

Ulysses chuckled obscenely. "Why, there something wrong with me killin' a lawman with . . ."

Whatever Ulysses was about to add was interrupted with a loud grunt followed by the unmistakable sound of his body striking the floor.

"Get out of here!" Rick hissed. A moment later, one of the women hurried out the door and raced down to another room where she disappeared.

Ben stepped into the doorway and saw Rick bending over his father. "What happened?"

"Couldn't you hear? I pistol-whipped him." Rick examined his father's scalp, then reached for Ulysses' pants and shirt. "That jail of yours had better be solid or he'll tear it apart when he comes around."

Ben did not waste any time as he helped Rick dress the old man. When they had him decent, they hoisted him up to his feet. Ben dug his shoulder into the old man's belly, then lifted him off the ground and started for the door.

"Say, Ben?"

He turned.

Rick expelled a deep breath. "You take care of him over there. My father has a lot of enemies. Cowardly men who'd jump at the chance to shoot him to death if they thought they could get away with it without getting caught. I hold you responsible until after the trial."

"I'll take that responsibility," Ben grunted. Ulysses was heavy, but Ben hesitated a minute. "I expect I owe you my thanks."

"Don't bother worrying about it. I did what I had to do to keep my blood brother and my father from killing each other. I figure you understand."

"I do," Ben told him as he headed for the stairs.

Making his way down carefully, Ben felt the eyes of every man in the room probing him as he carried Ulysses across the room and then outside. They were probably thinking he'd somehow managed to trick old Ulysses and then pistol-whip him.

Let them think that, Ben decided, remembering how Sheriff Nye had always maintained that a good lawman should build a reputation that would buffalo most would-be troublemakers. Besides that, the real test of his ability would come when Ulysses awoke and then realized that, for the first time in his life, he stood a good chance of being sentenced either to prison or maybe even to the gallows.

Three weeks later, Ben was present at Ulysses' trial as Rick walked up to the front of the courtroom, placed his left hand on the Bible and raised his right hand as the bailiff intoned, "Do you, Rick Kilbane, solemnly swear to tell the truth, the whole truth, so help you God?"

"I do," Rick said.

"Witness may take his seat," the judge pronounced.

Ulysses' lawyer, a slick-talking fellow named Maxwell Billingston, said, "Now, Mr. Kilbane. As you saw the shootings, please relate them to the judge."

"Very well," Rick replied. "The two deceased who were

shot during the poker game accused my father of cheating. They drew guns and were going to shoot him down in cold blood. There was no question about that."

"Objection," the prosecuting attorney shouted. "We've already heard that they demanded that Ulysses Kilbane roll up his sleeve. They had every reason to believe Mr. Kilbane was cheating them at cards. And since Ulysses is a known cheat . . ."

"Objection!" Billingston snapped. "Your honor, surely that kind of prejudicial remark should be struck from the record and . . ."

"Objection sustained," Judge Stuart Potter declared. "And I will hear no more slanderous talk from you, sir! That was entirely out of order in my court."

The prosecutor slumped back to his chair. Rick looked very confident. His white shirt, starched collar and expensive coat told everyone that he was a successful man. One who deserved their trust. To Ben, Rick seemed more like an actor on stage than someone whose father was on trial for murder.

Rick's eyes studied the packed courtroom as he continued. "Well, your honor, I had no choice but to intervene. I pulled my gun, and just when I was about to ask those men to drop their weapons, they must have decided to shoot. The next thing I knew, they were firing and my father was trying to defend his life. Fortunately, he was the better shootist."

"Objection!" the prosecuting attorney cried. "We've already heard several witnesses testify—under oath—that those two men were gunned down *after they were disarmed*. Your honor, please, can't we have some integrity in these proceedings!"

The judge colored red. "Sir, one more slanderous outburst

from you and I'll have the bailiff forcibly remove you from
this courtroom!"

The prosecutor sat down again. He looked over at Mandy,
and then at Ben who could not take his eyes off his blood
brother who was saying things that could not possibly be true.

Rick expelled a deep breath. "And as for the death of the
sheriff, well, everyone in Virginia City knows that Sheriff Nye
hated my father. He came into the Silver Dollar Saloon determined to kill Ulysses. The moment he walked into our estab-
lishment, he had his gun in his fist, saying he knew my father
was a murderer—a charge that he'd made publicly many
times. He dared my father to draw his weapon so that he
could save the citizens of Virginia City the cost of this trial."

Judge Potter held up his hand. "The sheriff actually said
this?"

"Yes sir," Rick said. "Sheriff Nye dared my father to pull a
derringer or a knife so that he could have a legal excuse to kill
him and save taxpayer money."

Ben ran his fingers through his hair and stifled a groan of
dismay. If this part were true, then it was because Sheriff Nye
had been trying to keep Ulysses from becoming reckless. And
yet, coming from Rick, it sounded like Nye had had some sort
of vendetta against Ulysses. The sad truth of the matter was,
maybe he had.

"Go on," Potter said.

"Well, I could see that my father was a dead man unless
something happened quick. Our bartender must have seen it
too because he bravely grabbed a shotgun from behind the
bar. He was a good, decent family man, and when he tried to
get the drop on Sheriff Nye and make him listen to reason,
Nye shot him right between the eyes."

Mandy was on her feet along with the prosecutor and both were shouting in protest. Mandy had tears streaming down her cheeks and the courtroom was in an uproar.

Potter banged his gavel down hard and shouted for order. Finally, he yelled something to the bailiff, who grabbed the prosecutor and forced him out of the room. It was a good five minutes before order was restored, and when the room fell silent, Ben could hear Mandy crying.

The judge leaned out from his bench. "If anyone—anyone at all—interrupts this court one more time, they will not only be removed, they will be jailed. Deputy Pope, do you understand me?"

Ben had been staring at Rick, but now he turned to the judge and nodded.

"Mr. Kilbane," Potter said, "you may continue your testimony."

Rick stared down at his hands. "I was shocked when Sheriff Nye shot our bartender. Only then did I realize that the sheriff had become mentally unbalanced. That he was committed to killing my father."

"That's a lie!" Ben said, bouncing to his own feet. "Sheriff Nye was the finest lawman in Nevada. Sure he hated Ulysses Kilbane! The man has killed time and time again, always with the excuse that it was in self-defense. And now . . ."

Potter banged his gavel down hard. "Deputy, we've already heard your sworn testimony and you are out of order. I am disgusted that a lawman has so little regard for the proceedings of a court of law that he would entirely disregard its order and interrupt testimony. Now sit down and do not interrupt again or I'll have *you* arrested!"

But Ben would *not* sit down. He raised his hand and

pointed an accusing finger at Rick. "I always believed in you," he said in a voice that trembled. "I never believed I'd see you do a thing like this. You're a liar, Rick. You're nothing but a goddamn liar!"

Rick turned white in the face. He came to his feet and shouted, "And you're a fool! I saved your life in that saloon!"

The judge began to pound his gavel down harder as the courtroom was filled with the sounds of men arguing both for and against Ulysses. Ben turned and hurried out of the courtroom before he lost control and went for Rick's throat.

Mandy had been on the mark, right from the start. Rick was no damned good. When the chips were down, he'd perjured himself to save his father. To do that, he'd slandered Sheriff Nye's good name. Told lies against a brave man who had fallen in the line of duty and could no longer defend his honor.

Ben started walking. He felt dead inside, just as his loyalty to Rick had died moments before in the courtroom.

"Ben!"

It was Mandy, and when he turned, he saw the tears streaming down her cheeks. She threw herself into his arms and sobbed. "It's fixed, all fixed. Potter has been bought and paid for, and my father has died for nothing!"

Ben wanted to tell Mandy that she was wrong. But he could not, so he just held her in his arms until she stopped crying, and then they walked slowly out to the cemetery to stand before Nye's grave.

And as the sun was sinking in the west, Ben glanced at it and vowed, "I'll get Ulysses, Sheriff. One way or another, I'll get him for you."

Mandy looked up at him and her thoughts were no longer

on Ulysses. That evil old man was going to be set free this time. What really concerned Mandy was Rick. Rick who had shown his true colors. Rick who had sold out to his father and for all the money that the Silver Dollar Saloon was making for the Kilbanes. But when she saw the set of Ben's jaw and the hard expression he bore, Mandy said nothing. She remembered her nightmare and shuddered.

"Why don't we just leave the Comstock? We could be married and maybe buy that farm you always wanted in California."

"No!" Ben lowered his voice. "I've got to finish this for your father and for myself. I've got to see it set right before I go."

Mandy pulled hard on his arm. "Stay and you'll wind up getting killed! Just like in my dream."

Ben turned and stared back at Virginia City. "I don't believe in dreams coming true—good ones or bad ones. All I believe in is honesty. Yesterday, I believed in honor and friendship. No more."

Mandy knelt beside her father's grave. "All I believe in is love," she said in a voice that was close to breaking. "And I love you."

CHAPTER TEN

Ben stood before the town council with his hat in his hand. He had shaved and gotten a bath and a haircut. His boots shone almost as brightly as his deputy's badge and he knew that he made a good impression on the five men who had invited him to a closed-door session which would determine his future.

Mr. Oscar Peterson, the mayor and head of the city council, was a jowly, pleasant banker. Like the others, he smoked a big cigar and dressed in a manner befitting his importance in Virginia City.

"Sit down, Ben," he said. "I know I speak for the entire city council when I say that you have been doing a fine job as acting sheriff these past few months."

"Thank you, sir." Ben smiled. "Sheriff Nye was a good teacher."

"Yes," Peterson said, puffing up a little because of what he was about to say. "You'll be happy to know that, just a few minutes ago, this council agreed to pay his widow fifty dollars a month for as long as she shall live."

Ben was pleased. "She'll be very grateful."

"Yes," the banker said, "we feel certain that she will be. And by the way, I understand that you and Miss Nye are engaged to be married!"

"That's true," Ben said and then added, "Of course, it's a little hard on a deputy's pay."

Peterson puffed a little more rapidly on his cigar. "We understand. That's the main reason we have called you before us today. What are you earning right now?"

The mayor knew very well what he was earning, but Ben played the game and told him anyhow. "Thirty dollars a month as acting sheriff."

"Is that sufficient to support a wife?"

"Yes sir. I couldn't have done it on a deputy's pay, but . . ."

Peterson cleared his throat. "And you shouldn't have to scrimp. I'm sure that you've won several thousand dollars in the ring and I know how popular you are with the fight fans here in Virginia City."

"I've done well enough," Ben admitted. "But fighting is a good way to get your brains beat out. I figure to stop fighting once I get married."

"What a shame," Peterson said. "You're still a young man coming into your prime."

"I'll have a wife to look after. Miss Nye doesn't abide with fighting and I can't say that I blame her."

"But it does pay good money," Peterson said, emphasizing his point heavily. "And a deputy's pay, as you reminded us, is hardly a living."

"That's why I intend to become sheriff—with your approval," Ben added quickly, smiling at the other members of the board.

Peterson looked down at some papers that were resting in a neat stack before him. "I'm afraid that does create a little bit of a problem for us, Ben."

"Sir?"

"Yes," Peterson continued, glancing toward his colleagues, who were obviously content to allow the mayor to do their talking. "You see, you have made no secret of your desire to fill Mr. Nye's shoes as permanent sheriff."

"No, I haven't. Like I said, I learned all I could from Sheriff Nye and . . ."

Peterson interrupted, "And yet, Sheriff Nye was gunned down just before he was about to shoot Mr. Kilbane, out of some kind of animosity that had developed between them."

"Now wait a minute! Sheriff Nye was killed in the act of making an arrest."

Peterson was no longer smiling around his cigar. "That's not what the evidence said or the judge ruled. You were present when Ulysses Kilbane was acquitted of all charges, making your arrest meaningless. And I'll come right out and tell you that Ulysses happens to be a very solid businessman who has supported every charity and public fund-raising effort we've ever had in Virginia City."

Ben expelled a deep breath. "Why don't you get to the point of my being here. Are you going to appoint me sheriff . . . or not?"

Peterson laid his cigar in an ashtray and steepled his fingers. He wore a big diamond ring and his cuff links were solid gold. After a moment of silence, he looked up at Ben and said, "I'll bet you've heard plenty about the legendary fighter, Kokomo Kelly."

"Of course I have. He was a prizefighter back East, then went down to Texas and became a Ranger before he settled into being a town sheriff. I heard he never stayed more than a couple of years in one place before he moved on."

"That's exactly right! And the thing of it is, Ben, we've got some major problems here on the Comstock. Kokomo Kelly is now a United States Marshal and he's available to work the Comstock from Silver City on over the divide to include our own Virginia City. He's expensive, but Silver City and Gold Hill will join us in sharing the burden of his salary."

"What about a sheriff?"

"We think we can cut costs and save the taxpayers' money by sharing Kokomo Kelly until he moves on."

"That's the stupidest thing I ever heard of!" Ben swore. "This town is too big to share its lawman with anyone. Virginia City needs a full-time sheriff."

"We disagree, Ben."

Ben clenched his fists at his side as the mayor continued. "Listen, Ben, it's our opinion that Kelly can clean up things around here in a year or two and then we feel confident that you can step in and take charge. You're still a little green for this big a job and we want you to stay on as Kelly's deputy. You know this town and you'd be a big help to the man. We'll up your salary to twenty-five a month. You also have my word that, when Kelly moves on, you're his replacement. And I think you know that a United States Marshal makes considerably more than a town sheriff."

"To hell with it!" Ben swore, unpinning his badge and laying it before the mayor. "I'll be damned if I'll nursemaid some old geezer who should have been put out to pasture ten or twenty years ago!"

Suddenly, the back door opened and a tall man in his sixties stepped inside. "My name is Kokomo Kelly, son, and this old geezer knows more about trouble and sheriffin' that you probably will, even if you spend a lifetime swappin' lead with outlaws. I ain't ready for no damned pasture yet, unless you think you might like to try and put me there."

Ben stared at the man who was as tall as he was, and as lean and tough-looking as a strip of rawhide. Ben peered right into his pale eyes and learned in an instant that Kokomo Kelly didn't know the meaning of a bluff. He had the look about him of a man who would take a punch or a bullet in order to deliver the same. The old town-tamer wore his hair and his mustache long and silver. He was dressed in a black frocked coat with buckskin breeches and on his narrow hip was the fanciest pair of guns that Ben had ever seen.

Kokomo was burned by the insults he'd heard. "Well, Deputy Pope, what's the matter with your tongue now? You want to fight? I'll fight you. Guns, fists, knives . . . hell, we can fight with clubs or rocks! Doesn't matter to me. I'll win, no matter what you choose."

Ben outweighed Kokomo by sixty pounds of muscle and he had no fear of getting whipped in a fistfight, even though Kokomo was probably still the faster man with a sixgun. "I apologize for my words, Mr. Kelly. I meant no offense, but I figure I was owed this job."

Kokomo's eyes darted to the council, then returned to Ben. "It appears you figured wrong. I like big, tough deputies that can take orders. You're big, but are you willin' to do as I say and work for me? If not, I'll find someone who can."

"How long will you stay on the Comstock?"

"As long as it takes to clean it up."

"And will you recommend I be appointed a United States Marshal up here when you leave?"

"How should I know! Ask me before I leave."

Ben frowned. "All right," he said at last. "I'll stay and be your deputy."

"Good!" Kokomo snapped. "Now pin that badge back on your broad chest and let's go make the rounds. You'll be introducing me to a lot of folks before this day is done."

Despite his disappointment at not being named sheriff, Ben thought he was going to enjoy Kokomo Kelly. The man had a gruff but direct way about him that suited a frontier lawman, and his personality and manner were reminiscent of Sheriff Nye, though the two were outwardly quite different. Nye had been unimposing, while this man would have attracted the same kind of attention as Buffalo Bill. Kokomo Kelly had a swagger and the appearance of a showman, while Nye had been as common-looking as grass until he was aroused to action.

They started their rounds at the north end of C Street by the Union Brewery and worked their way south to the firehouse, then crossed the street to the Old Washoe Club and made a loop. Ben introduced Kelly as the new United States Marshal to every businessman on the block. When they came to the Silver Dollar Saloon, Kelly pushed out his arm and said, "It appears to me that going inside there might be unhealthy for you."

"It comes with the job."

"Have you been inside since the trial?"

Ben was ashamed to say that he had not. "I've had no call to, but I might as well let them know that I'm not afraid."

"Suit yourself," Kokomo said. "But I've heard all about Ulysses and Rick Kilbane, and I guess they're the ones that have to be dealt with, sooner or later. Frankly, I'd rather it be later. So just stay close to the door and keep your eyes and ears open for trouble."

Ben nodded, then followed the marshal inside.

Nothing had changed, even the customers were the same ones who'd been drinking the afternoon that Nye was gunned down. Ben saw Rick and Jenny at the same table and Ulysses was at his favorite back table reading the *Territorial Enterprise* when Kokomo said, "That him?"

"Yeah."

"Looks as mean as a lobo wolf, don't he?" Kokomo asked under his breath.

"Meaner," Ben replied, his eyes on Rick, who had stopped talking to Jenny the moment he'd stepped inside.

Ben had not spoken to Rick since the trial. He'd seen his old friend on the street and once riding out of town with Jenny French in a buggy. But except for eye contact, nothing had passed between them. Now, however, he felt compelled to speak to his ex-friend, if only to set the ground rules between them, so there would be no misunderstanding.

He waited until Kokomo had joined Ulysses and then he walked over to Rick and touched his hat. "Afternoon," he said stiffly.

"Afternoon, Deputy." Rick's appraisal was cool and detached. "You lost or something?"

Ben felt his cheeks warm. "No, I'm just taking our new United States Marshal around for introductions. Miss French, you're looking as pretty as ever."

Jenny smiled and relaxed. "And I hear that you're engaged to marry Miss Nye. Congratulations."

"Thank you."

Ben returned his attention to Rick. The man appeared different, causing Ben to wonder if people looked the way you felt about them. "We got a new marshal."

"So I gather," Rick said. He paused for a moment, then added, "I'll say this, I've got to hand it to you for having the nerve to come in here after calling me and my father liars in Judge Potter's courtroom."

Ben was quick to his own defense. "You knew the sheriff was my friend but you and your pa killed him all the same."

"He came looking for a bullet," Rick said between clenched teeth. "He got what he wanted. Now, what do *you* want?"

"Nothing," Ben heard himself say. "At least, not today."

"Then get the hell out of my sight."

"Rick, stop it!" Jenny cried. "Ben is your friend!"

"*Was* my friend. Let it be, Jenny."

"But I won't! If you don't settle this, something terrible could happen between you."

Rick spun on Jenny and slapped her across the mouth with the back of his hand. "I said to leave be what is none of your business!"

Ben was as stunned as Jenny by Rick's sudden violence. Jenny shook her head, then slowly came out of her seat. "You've changed too much," she whispered. "Something good died inside of you the day that you helped your father gun down Sheriff Nye."

"Shut up!"

"I'm quitting you," Jenny said. "I'm leaving the Comstock."

"The hell you are!"

Rick grabbed for her, but Jenny was already out of his reach and heading for the stairs. "Don't try to stop me!" she called.

For a moment, Rick seemed caught up in his own indecision. Then he yelled for the bartender to bring him a bottle.

"What happened to you?" Ben asked him in a quiet voice. "What went wrong?"

Rick chuckled to himself and it wasn't a pretty sound. "You know, I liked you a hell of a lot better when you were a drunk, Ben. At least you were humorous then. Now . . . now you're just a pain in the ass. An itch to be scratched. Why don't you get smart? Marry and leave the Comstock before I wind up putting you out of your misery."

"I got a job to finish and you're part of it," Ben said. "You had me fooled when you arrested your pa for me. Had me fooled right up until your testimony. Only then did I realize you'd played me for a sucker in order to get your father off without a sentence."

Rick suddenly shoved his chair back so hard that it scraped across the floor and captured everyone's attention. His gun hand stayed near his holster and he used his other hand to point at Ben. When he spoke, his voice was ragged with pent-up fury.

"The past is done and buried," he said. "Tread on me or my father again, and I'll see you planted on Boot Hill, alongside of Nye and anyone else who comes around sticking his nose where he shouldn't."

"I understand. Thanks for the warning."

"Now get out of here!"

"I think I'll wait for Jenny," he said. "And Marshall Kokomo Kelly. Maybe you've heard of him?"

The bartender came hurrying over with a bottle.

"I have," Rick said. "And he'll get the same as Nye did if he tries to send my father to the gallows. Get out of town,

Ben! You once said you wanted to be a dirt farmer. Then go and be one!"

"Not until this is finished."

"Meaning my father and me. Isn't that right?"

Ben found himself nodding his head. "Yeah," he said. "I guess so."

Rick started to say something, but stopped when Jenny came hurrying down the stairs from their room. She had one carpetbag stuffed with things and she was crying as she rushed across the saloon and then out the door.

"Now see what you've done," Rick said bitterly as he poured himself a drink and threw it down with a vengeance.

"Not me," Ben replied. "For that, you can take all the credit yourself."

Kokomo Kelly's voice raised in anger. "You killed Sheriff Nye and I'm here to say that you're gonna pay with your own blood the next time you shoot someone in this town!"

Ulysses lunged at the marshal, and faster than anything, Kokomo grabbed a bottle off his table and bashed the old gambler across his forehead so hard the bottle shattered. Ulysses went down howling and clutching his face.

Rick's hand streaked for his gun, but Ben anticipated the move and his fist smashed into Rick's jaw, knocking him to the floor. Before Rick could recover, Ben disarmed him.

"I think it's time we said good-bye for now," Kokomo said, his own gun out as he retreated toward the front door. "Come on, Deputy."

Ben needed no further urging. One thing was immediately obvious for anyone to see—Kokomo Kelly was not a man who wasted time shaking hands and making new friends.

CHAPTER ELEVEN

Ben stood beside Jenny French while the stagecoach driver loaded bags and suitcases and the passengers waited impatiently for a late departure. During the past hour they had not spoken a dozen words, but now that the stage was almost ready to leave, Jenny wanted to tell everything about Rick Kilbane.

"He has changed so much since his father gunned down Sheriff Nye. When I first met him, he was different from Ulysses. Sure, I knew he was forceful and ambitious, but he was also kind and honest. He had a sense of justice that I admired, because you almost never see it in handsome young men with money."

"Was it Sheriff Nye's death that changed him so much?"

"Mostly," Jenny said. "But just being around his father was like taking a daily dose of poison. For a long, long time, he resisted Ulysses. He refused to cheat at cards and I often saw him pass money on the sly to someone down on their luck. He was, as you might say, a 'soft touch' despite the Kilbane reputation that his father insisted they uphold."

Jenny shrugged her shoulders hopelessly. "I begged him to leave the Comstock. We could have gone away together and lived a decent life. I have some savings and so does Rick. We didn't need his half interest in the saloon. But he wouldn't believe me. He was, despite all his cockiness, still unsure of himself. He needed to get away from his father and prove to himself that he could succeed on his own."

Ben shook his head. "Rick succeeded at anything he ever tried. Everything comes easy for him."

"Maybe that's his real curse," Jenny said. "He's never known hard times. Never had to do manual work or fret about where he was going to find the money to buy his next meal."

"Yes," Ben said. "But living in a saloon, he's seen plenty of the downside of life. He knows how rough things can get. I guess maybe that's why he's taken the easy way out."

"But it *isn't* the easy way! It'll bring him down, just as sure as it will his father."

The stagecoach driver climbed up into his seat. "Everybody that's goin' to Reno had better get on board!" he called as the passengers hurried forward to get the window seats.

"You'd better go," Ben said. "That coach only carries six and there won't be another out until tomorrow."

Jenny hugged his neck. "I love Rick! I think I always will. He's your blood brother, so you can't give up on him!"

Ben didn't quite know what to say as he held Jenny for a moment, before she pulled away and said, "I've a brother who has a thriving newspaper in Denver in addition to several other little businesses. He's been after me for years to come live with him and his wife. To become an honest woman doing a nine-to-five job."

Jenny tried to smile but failed miserably. "I don't know if I can do it, but I'm going to try."

"You'll do fine. Forget about Rick and find a prosperous young man to marry. Raise children, be happy."

"You do the same with Miss Nye," she said as he helped her up into the coach.

Ben watched her dab at her eyes and he waved as the driver cracked his whip and the coach pulled away. He turned to see Rick standing outside the Silver Dollar Saloon, and though he was two blocks away, Ben sensed the man's loss. Rick had always stood straight and tall, but when the stagecoach disappeared from sight, he turned and went back inside as bent as an old man.

Ben did not see Rick for two months while he tried to work under the new marshal. Working under Kokomo Kelly was unlike anything that Ben could have imagined. The old town-tamer was irascible, unpredictable and always entertaining. He was, Ben discovered, a very careful man, especially when it came to his own health and welfare.

The first example Ben had of this was when they were walking down C Street late one evening and they heard gunfire in the Bucket of Blood Saloon. Ben drew his sixgun and started to rush forward, but Kokomo grabbed his arm and dug in heels.

"Hang on now!" Kokomo said as Ben tried to shake the marshal free. "The worst thing in the world for a lawman to do is to go barrelin' into a gunfight."

Ben listened to the shots. "But people are killing each other in there! We've got to stop them!"

"They'll stop themselves plenty soon enough. Either they'll come to their senses and realize they're playing for keeps, or else someone will die and that'll end the fuss. Either way, a smart lawman always waits until the shootin' is finished."

"But . . ."

"But nothing!" Kokomo said angrily. "Why, if you go

bustin' in there half-cocked, you'll probably get ventilated. And even if you don't, what are you going to do?"

"Make an arrest!"

"On who? You don't know the innocent from the guilty." Kokomo pried the gun out of Ben's hand. "A long time back, when I was young and foolish like you appear to be, I did exactly what you were about to do. And you know what, I arrested the first man I saw. Like a fool, I pointed my damn sixgun at him and told him to drop his weapon and stand up. He did and the fella he was feudin' with shot him to death!"

"Give me back my gun," Ben said.

"You going to wait until I say to go in there?"

"Yeah."

Kokomo handed him back his gun and they stood out in the street listening to the shooting. "Must be four or five shootin' the hell outa that saloon," Kokomo said, as they heard the back-bar mirror shatter and fall, and then saw the big front window explode with gunshots and shower across the boardwalk.

"They're destroying the place!" Ben cried.

"It's only money," Kokomo said, rolling a cigarette. "Sure ain't worth spillin' *our* blood over."

Ben was totally exasperated. "When you took the oath of office, you must have sworn to protect life *and* property."

"I don't seem to recollect the property part," the marshal said, scratching a match on his holster and frowning as he inhaled the cheap tobacco he favored. "At any rate, this shootin' business rarely lasts more than a couple of minutes. Someone is bound to either take one in the brisket or else start wavin' a white flag. Deputy, you just relax and live a little longer."

It was hard for Ben to relax. Sheriff Nye would have plowed into the Bucket of Blood and settled this business straightaway!

About the time that Kokomo Kelly finished his cigarette and ground the butt under his heel, the shooting stopped.

"Are we finally going in there now?" Ben asked impatiently.

"Uh-huh," Kokomo said. "I think the issue is probably settled by now. But just in case the winners think that the losers might have a few friends coming to the rescue, I'd be careful about busting in there unannounced."

Ben hurried on ahead thinking that Kokomo's advice might not be all wrong. When he reached the bat-wing saloon doors, he hollered, "It's Deputy Pope and Marshal Kelly comin' in! Everybody throw their guns on the floor and raise your hands high!"

Ben heard guns hit the floor and then he entered cautiously with Kokomo at his flank whispering, "You're learning how to save your hide, Deputy. Listen to me and you might live to be as old as I am."

Ben said nothing as he entered the saloon to witness the carnage. There was busted glass everywhere and two dead men sprawled out on the floor. Another was badly wounded and three more were standing behind the bullet-riddled bar with their hands up in the air.

"Christamighty!" Ben whispered, surveying the devastation. "What happened in here?"

"They started it!" one of the men behind the bar stammered. "And by gawd, we upped and finished it!"

"What was the fight over!" Ben demanded.

"They said we worked for the worst mine on the Comstock

that hired nothin' but third-rate fellas which didn't know one end of a fuse from the other!"

"Well, there isn't any difference between one end . . ."

Kokomo didn't want to hear any barroom explanations. "Save it for the judge. You and your friends are under arrest. Let's take a walk to the jail."

Now that the killing was done, the three surviving miners acted as docile as rabbits. They nodded their heads and marched single file out of the saloon like first-year schoolchildren.

"Call for a doctor," Kokomo said as he herded the men out of the door, "and if that one with the bullet in his chest lives, tell him he's under arrest the same as these boys. And you better send for a mortician."

Ben stayed at the saloon until the mortician arrived and then he helped carry the dead men to the funeral parlor. They were young; one did not look to be out of his teens.

"Who is going to pay for my services?" the mortician asked.

Ben searched through the dead men's pockets but found only a cheap pocket watch, a couple of jacknives and some loose change. "I guess the county will have to foot the bill if none of their friends comes forward or offers to take up a collection."

The mortician was a small, tidy man with an unfailingly sour disposition. "Dead men have no friends on the Comstock," he complained. "I'll put 'em in cheap pine boxes and have a boy cut their names in a wooden cross. What are their names?"

"I don't know but I'll find out for you," Ben promised. He

stopped at the door and looked back at the pair. "They died for hardly any reason at all."

The mortician looked at him. "Since when did fools and miners need a good reason to die?"

Ben left without a word. He went back to the Bucket of Blood and watched the doctor try to save the life of the miner with a bullet in his chest. The man's face was the color of wax and he was struggling hard to breathe. Each gasp had a gurgling sound to it, and Ben knew that the poor fellow was a goner because he was shot through the lungs.

"He's done for, only he won't quit," the doctor said with a sad shake of his head. "What was the argument about?"

"The usual differences of opinion," Ben replied. "Nothing new or important."

"These fools seem to go out of their way to kill or be killed," the doctor grunted, climbing back to his feet. He snapped his medical bag shut and started to walk away.

"Hey! You just going to leave him?"

The doctor stopped, turned and said, "I can't do anything to help him now. Better you call a priest or a minister. Give him a drink of whiskey if you want. He's a goner, no matter what anyone does."

After the doctor left, Ben sent for the Reverend Walters who came and gave the man his last rites as the saloon's customers took turns buying the dying man drinks which they carefully poured down his gullet. It took the miner nearly an hour to die and he must have had twenty or thirty shots of whiskey poured down his throat. He was smiling when he gave up the fight and everyone agreed he was probably very drunk, but at least, where he was going, he wouldn't have to worry about a hangover.

When the miner died, Ben went back to the sheriff's office and explained what had happened.

"Well," Kokomo snapped, "that's a damn disappointment. I was hoping that one would at least pull through. Would have helped us a little."

"How do you mean?"

The marshal led Ben outside where they could not be overheard by the new prisoners. "I mean that we get a dollar a day for each prisoner and these men will be here nearly a month before the trial is over. Now, if it only costs fifty cents a day to feed them, that means we get the other fifty cents to keep ourselves!"

"But as high as prices are on the Comstock, you can't feed a dog for fifty cents a day!"

The marshal's face screwed up with exasperation. "Aw, sure you can. Lots of porridge, plenty of good, nourishing soup. I've already made a deal with a couple of restaurants for their table scraps. We can even get it down lower'n fifty cents, I'll bet."

"Seems dishonest and shifty to me," Ben said stubbornly. "I mean, if we are paid a dollar to feed them, then that's how we ought to spend the dollar."

Kokomo Kelly puffed up like a bullfrog and his face got stormy. "Listen, Deputy, we risk our lives to protect the citizens of this territory. And we do it for damn little thanks and even less pay. So when we see a little opportunity to turn an extra dollar or two, then we take advantage of the situation. Is that understood?"

"I guess so!" Ben snapped. "But you sure operate in a way that leaves some questions in my mind."

"Question all you want! I don't care. You're young and still stupid. When you get to be my age—if you don't get shot, which is a *big* if—then you'll see that taking care of yourself is more important than taking care of a bunch of city fathers and blowhards who expect everything and are willing to pay almost nothing."

Kokomo's eyes sparked. "Oh, son, I've seen it all! Every town council that ever lived was nothing but a bunch of stuffed shirts, always toadying around showing off their gold watches, and then when it comes to paying a lawman a fair wage, they act poorer than parsons. You'll see."

Ben needed time to think. He went outside and walked up toward Sun Mountain. He looked up at the summit and even considered the benefits of a good climb to its peak and the fine view he would behold. But instead, he turned and walked back down to Mandy's place. She worked in a millinery store, but it was past closing time and so he knew she'd be at home with her mother.

"I was hoping you'd stop by," she said, coming to the gate and walking him to her porch where they sat in a swing. "I heard the shooting in the Bucket of Blood and saw you carting out a couple of dead men. I'm sorry that sort of thing happens so often."

Ben told her about how Marshal Kelly had smoked a cigarette outside while the shooting had run its course. He was too embarrassed to tell her how Kokomo Kelly planned to skim fifty cents a day off each prisoner's food. "But I still can't believe we just waited while that gun battle roared on and on."

"Marshal Kelly is a wise man," Mandy said. "I think he's right. If my father had been a little slower, a little more deliberate, he might still be alive."

Mandy's mother brought them some lemonade, and after she had gone back inside, Ben said, "She's starting to smile again. Starting to look like she might decide life is worth living. But she still disapproves of me."

"It's not you; it's the fact that you're a lawman. She spent years telling me never to marry a military man or a law officer. And now, I'm engaged to one. She likes you personally, she's just worried sick that I'll become a widow some day."

"Yeah," Ben said. "I knew that was the reason. But I won't always wear a badge. Anyway, it's good to see that she looks so much better."

"It's taken time," Mandy said, "but I think she's accepted the fact that Father is dead. She always said he'd never reach old age. I remember her begging him to quit being a lawman. But he just couldn't."

"It gets in your blood," Ben said.

"What about farming in California? Ben, you promised me you'd quit fighting in the ring. Promise me you'll quit the law tomorrow and take me to California."

"With what?" he sighed. "I've barely got enough money to feed and clothe myself. Like most everyone else on the Comstock, I've bought some mining stock. So far, none of it has paid off."

"But it might."

"Sure," Ben said, "and it might not. The thing of it is, a California farm costs a lot of money. You have to buy livestock and farm equipment. A house, seed and . . ."

"Stop worrying," she said.

"All right. But what I dream of costs a lot of money and I can't seem to save any money."

"And you won't if you continue being a deputy."

"That's true," he said. "And I can't be a miner. So it doesn't leave me with much to offer."

Mandy hugged his neck. "I've passed up offers to marry a banker and an attorney, and I did it because I think you've got more to offer than anyone else I know. Besides, you captured my imagination when you said you'd take me to California and we'd farm. Do you know very much about farming?"

"Well, sort of. I read the *Farmer's Almanac* and the *Farmer's Gazette*. Read them from cover to cover. I plan to raise corn, cotton and oats in California."

Mandy squeezed his big hand. "Let's get married right away. Mother wants to leave too. She'll sell this house and get a couple of hundred dollars for it. We could all go to California and make a new start."

Ben shook his head emphatically. "And leave Ulysses Kilbane a free man after gunning down your father. No, I just won't do it!"

The expectancy drained out of Mandy's face. "I know you won't," she said quietly. "But my father is dead. We have to let the past go. You, me and especially my mother. And the best way to do that is to get a fresh start somewhere else. This is no place to be for us. It's nothing but a godforsaken boomtown. A dusty, dirty, freezing, sweating, treeless boomtown. And even if it is the biggest strike in history, it will go bust someday and all this will become worthless. Only a few rich investors, a couple of exceptionally lucky miners will reap any lasting rewards. All the Comstock will do is take our lives and leave us empty and old."

"I better get back to the office," Ben said, standing up. "I'll see you tomorrow evening after work."

Mandy nodded, but her voice had a new edge of determination. "I won't stay here waiting for you until either you kill Ulysses or he kills you. I deserve better than that, Ben. You're going to have to make up your mind. Do you want my love . . . or your own revenge? I don't think you've got time to have them both."

Ben dipped his chin and walked away.

CHAPTER TWELVE

Rick Kilbane could feel anger flowing through him like liquid heat. He was losing money fast. The two men who sat across from him at the poker table were experienced professionals. They were also poor winners.

"It just isn't your day," the one named Colton gloated. "I'd heard that you were as good as old Ulysses, but you ain't. In fact, you ain't worth a damn."

The other man named Modesto grinned. He was heavyset, thirtyish, with penetrating eyes and porcine lips. He blew smoke in Rick's face when he laughed, which was every time he won a hand. And he won often.

Rick could not figure it out. Either Colton and Modesto were sending signals back and forth in a way he had not discovered, or else they were very good and very lucky. Rick wasn't sure which. Because of the Kilbane reputation for killing cheats, few men were bold enough to try using a marked deck or some elaborate means of beating the house. But these were bold men and they were very confident.

"Why don't you get Ulysses down here?" Modesto said, glancing toward the stairs.

"I told you," Rick said. "He's not feeling well."

"He's drunk is what he is," Colton said with a smirk on his lean face. "Hell, kid, ain't nothing new for Ulysses."

Rick pushed back his chair and stood up. "I need another drink," he said.

Colton grabbed the bottle of whiskey resting between them. "What's wrong with drinking some of ours?"

"I like to buy my own," Rick said, turning his back on the pair and walking over to the bar.

He whispered to the bartender, "Give me a beer now, and when it's empty, bring me another and spill it on the cards we're using. Then apologize and bring me one of those fresh decks that pa keeps for the big games."

The bartender nodded impassively and poured Rick a beer. Fifteen minutes later, Rick's glass was empty and the bartender brought over another beer and dutifully spilled it across the table. He did it with just the touch of a seasoned actor.

"Well, goddamn you!" Colton swore, pushing back from the table and wiping beer from his clothes. "You ruined the deck!"

"I'm sorry, sir!" The bartender looked aghast at what he had done. He mopped at the table, looking as if he expected to be backhanded by one of the players. "I am very sorry, gentlemen."

"Do that again," Rick said, "and you're fired!"

"Let's move over to the next table," Modesto said, glaring at the bartender.

But Colton objected. "This is a lucky table for me. I want to stay right here."

Rick knew he had to object. Colton was a little suspicious. "I think we ought to move."

"No," Colton said. "Either we keep playing right here, or I quit."

Rick shrugged and said, "You win."

The bartender hurried off and returned with a fresh deck. He set it down in the middle of the table and Modesto picked the cards up and spent almost a full minute examining them. Finding nothing, he nodded to his partner and said, "Looks all right to me."

"Deal," Rick clipped. "I'm better than a thousand dollars down. I'm in a hurry to make it up."

Modesto cut the fresh deck which had been altered in New York City with such skill and artistry that it had cost Ulysses almost a hundred dollars. Each card had undergone a minute alteration in its back scrollwork. These alterations were often no more than a hundredth of an inch wide and it took hours of practice to detect, then memorize their locations. But once memorized, they enabled Rick to read his opponent's cards at a glance.

Rick lost three straight hands before he finally felt comfortable enough to win a pot with the new cards. It was a pot that added up to nearly a thousand dollars and he said, "So maybe my luck is going to change before I go broke."

"Don't count on it," Modesto said. "Deal!"

Rick dealt the cards and won again. He lost the next two hands, but since he could read his opponents' cards and knew when to fold early, his losses were minimal. He kept playing, losing a little, winning more and more. By early evening, the chips were back on his side of the table and the two professionals strongly suspected that they were being cheated, but they could not figure out how.

"Deal me out," Modesto said. "I don't like the way things are turning. Colton, I think we better cut our losses and quit."

"Not yet," Colton said. He leaned over the cards, staring at them. "Something is wrong here and I mean to figure it out plain before I quit. Our luck hasn't been the same since that bartender changed the deck."

Rick stiffened. "Your friend inspected them. Reinspect them if you want."

"I want," Colton said, scraping up the cards and coming to his feet.

There was a lamp overhead, and as Rick and the other saloon customers held their breath and waited, Colton studied the cards with the concentration of a jeweler looking into the heart of a precious stone. He ran his fingers over the edges, trying to feel a roughness to indicate that they were shaved. Satisfied that was not how the cards were marked, he turned them one way and then the other to see if he could find any indentations or thumbnail marks that had been used.

"Nothing!" he said in anger as he hurled the deck upon the table and glared at Rick. "All right, now stand up and take off that coat, then roll up your sleeves."

Rick stood up. His hand dropped beside his gun. "I haven't got any cards up my sleeves and there isn't a holdout either."

"I want to see for myself," Colton said.

"If that's your bet, it's going to cost you a bullet to see up my sleeve."

The two gamblers looked at each other, and then Modesto laughed as if nothing mattered. The laughter was still in his throat when Colton made his draw.

Rick had expected a distraction and he was ready. His hand streaked down and his sixgun leaped out of his holster in a smooth, unbroken motion. He beat Colton easily and shot him through his chest before he felt the impact of Modesto's bullet. He was knocked sideways, and as he was falling, Modesto hurried his shot and fired twice more but missed. Just as

Rick hit the floor, he fired again and placed a bullet right between Modesto's close-set eyes.

It happened so fast that no one in the Silver Dollar quite believed they saw Rick's draw. But his gun was smoking and two dead men lay at his feet. Rick reached out for a chair and pulled himself upright, then shrugged off his coat before rolling up his sleeves. "You heard what they said. And you can see that I am clean."

"You're shot," a man said.

Rick glanced at his left shoulder. It was a bad but certainly not a mortal wound. "What the hell is going on!" Ulysses shouted, pulling on his pants as he came halfway down the stairs.

Rick walked toward him. "There's nothing to be worried about, Pa. Go back to bed."

Ulysses stared at the smoke and the dead men. Satisfied, he looked to his son. "You got hit."

"Modesto was one of the fastest men I ever saw," Rick told his father. "I damn near made a fatal mistake in thinking that he was the slower of the two."

"Naw, hell no!" Ulysses grunted. "Colton was never that fast. But Modesto, he was sudden. You should have hit him first."

Rick walked over to the bar and the bartender handed him a towel which he used to staunch the flow of blood from his shoulder. He was already feeling a little light-headed. "Drinks on the house!"

Taking a deep pull on the whiskey, Rick grinned up at Ulysses who looked proud enough to burst his britches—if he ever got them belted around his middle.

"Nice piece of work!" Ulysses bellowed.

Rick nodded. He looked at himself in the mirror, and for some queer reason, he thought of Jenny French and the way that his life was unfolding.

Rick was still on his feet an hour after the doctor had bandaged his shoulder and ordered both him and Ulysses to stop drinking and go to bed. Surprisingly, Ulysses had followed the doctor's orders, but Rick was too wound up inside to sleep, so he stayed downstairs, talking with the saloon's customers, drinking round after round of whiskey until his head started to spin.

It was almost midnight when Marshal Kelly strode through the door. He had just climbed off his horse after riding up from Silver City where he and Ben had been making an arrest. Kokomo was in a bad mood and he was ready for trouble.

"You're under arrest," he said, grabbing Rick by his wounded shoulder and hauling him around.

Rick doubled up with pain, then quickly straightened. "Marshal, I got a roomful of witnesses that will testify that I used my gun in self-defense."

"I haven't got the time or the patience to question them," Kokomo growled.

"I've done nothing wrong!" Rick said, aware that he was slurring his words and facing a very dangerous man. "You can ask anybody here . . ."

At least a dozen men started talking all at once, but the marshal wasn't listening. "You Kilbanes are always killing people in self-defense, aren't you?"

Rick shook his head. He glanced up the stairs, but his father wasn't going to be there to help him.

"Look at me when I ask you a question!" the marshal snapped.

Rick took a deep breath. "I'm not going to jail," he said.

Kokomo Kelly stepped back and his hand shaded his gun. "Then I guess I'm within the law to shoot you if you're resisting arrest. Either come, or draw. It's your choice."

Rick could not believe this was happening. Not in the Silver Dollar Saloon with a crowd of people willing to testify he'd shot in self-defense. Not with Ulysses just upstairs.

But it was happening and through a whiskey haze, Rick penetrated the meaning of what was about to happen. *The marshal wanted him to draw.* Wanted to kill him while his mind was fogged with pain and whiskey.

"Oh no," he said, shaking the cobwebs from his head. "I won't draw on you!"

"Sure you will," the marshal said. "You've just killed two fast men and you've got thirty years on me. You can beat a slow old man to the draw. Come on!"

Rick threw his hands in the air, though the movement made him gasp with pain. "If you draw that gun, Marshal, it will be murder and you'll hang."

Kelly cursed him then. Called him names that Rick had not believed any man would ever call him and ended by saying, "You and your father are both cowards. You only play poker or use a gun when you've got the edge."

The bartender leaned across the bar. "Should I go bring Ulysses down," he asked.

"No!"

"Yes!" Kokomo Kelly said, raising his hand and slapping Rick across the face as the crowd looked on in stunned silence. "Tell Ulysses Kilbane I called him and his son a coward. Tell him to come on down right now."

The bartender started to move, but Rick reached across the

bar and grabbed him by the arm. "Stay put!" he grated. "Don't you see he wants to kill me and pa! This isn't the time!"

The white-faced bartender nodded with sudden under-standing. "Rick, your pa will have you out first thing in the morning. Don't you worry none. He'll tear that damn sheriff's office down and . . ."

"No!" Rick said. "That's exactly what this sonofabitch wants!"

Kokomo slapped him again and Rick felt his lips split as the lawman hurled another challenge at him. "There's still time to draw that fast gun of yours, kid. Go ahead and do it."

"I'm coming to jail," Rick said, wiping his lips with his sleeve. "I'm coming peacefully. Take my gun."

All the anger seemed to wash out of the marshal. For a moment, Rick thought the man was going to kill him where he stood, but instead, Kelly gave a sad shake of his head and disarmed him. "All right," he said, "let's take a walk."

Rick kept his hands up all the way to the jail cell. When the iron door clanged shut, he looked at one of the prisoners who was stretched out on the thin pallet and said, "Move."

The man moved and Rick stretched out and closed his eyes as Marshal Kelly watched him in sullen silence. "You're smarter than your father, I'll say that," Kokomo growled. "But brains won't keep me from killing you and your pa one of these days."

Rick turned his head toward the man. "Marshal, you're a dead man already, only you don't realize it."

Kelly's knuckles turned white as he gripped the cell bars and shook them in anger before he turned and walked away.

"Where's Deputy Pope!" Rick shouted.

"He's down in Silver City."

"Why didn't he come up to help you?"

"That's none of your damned business."

Rick chuckled. "Sure it is. You knew he wouldn't allow you to slap and insult me. You knew he'd keep you from trying to goad me into a gunfight."

"Shut up."

Rick smiled at the ceiling. "Next time you tell me to draw, I'll be dead sober, Marshal. And even if you get past me, my pa will kill you. The only chance you got is to grab your things and ride like hell for parts unknown. That's your *only* chance."

Kokomo came out of his chair. "You may be right, but a lot of men better than the Kilbanes have tried to kill me and failed. And consider this—what'll happen to Ben Pope if I'm shot down?"

The marshal came over to the cell and his eyes narrowed when he looked at his prisoner. "He still considers you a friend, despite everything you've done to prove otherwise. And I haven't been a lawman all these years without knowing a thing or two about how men think. You still consider him your friend too."

"Not anymore he isn't."

"Bullshit," the marshal snorted. "And how are you going to feel when your father kills him?"

The smile on Rick's lips slipped badly. "That won't happen."

"Oh no? Why? Do you think Ben is going to allow you and your pa to go on killing people?" Kokomo snorted. "You grew up with Ben and you know him better than I do. And even I know he'll come gunning for you and Ulysses if I go down and he becomes the sheriff of this town. If I don't shoot you first, sooner or later, he'll either kill you—or you'll have to kill him. Think about it."

Rick sat bolt upright because Kelly had it figured right. "So what's the answer?"

"Get off the Comstock before this goes any farther. It's that simple."

Rick stood up and walked over to the bars. "It's never that simple. If I go, you'll kill my father and then I'll have to come back and settle things."

Kokomo shrugged. "Hell, kid. Maybe that old devil's luck will hold and he'll kill me first, but that still leaves Ben as the new sheriff."

Rick returned to the bunk and lay down to ponder the Chinese riddle he was seemingly caught up in without any solution. He didn't give a damn about Marshal Kelly, but Ben was another matter.

Making up his mind, he again stood up and walked to the cell door. "If I give you my word that I'll leave town and not come back, will you let me go?"

Kelly thought about it for a minute. "Where are you bound?"

"Denver," he said before he even put thought to the answer.

"Yeah," Kelly said. "I heard about that pretty saloon girl that left you and went to Denver."

"What about my father?"

"What about him?" Kokomo asked. "Either way, when he sobers up and hears what I did to you in his own saloon, he's going to make it a point to kill me. Your staying or leaving won't change that."

"Promise me you'll give him a stand-up gunfight and not ambush him."

"I can't make any promises. We both know that one of us will be dead by this time tomorrow. He won't play by any rules and neither will I."

It was true. Ulysses might even hire someone as an assassin. "Okay," Rick said, "we got a deal."

The marshal came over and unlocked the cell. "I'll even let you go back to the Silver Dollar and collect your things and get some money if you promise to keep this to yourself and be out of this town in less than an hour."

Rick stepped out of the cell. "I hope you aren't planning to shoot me in the back when I go out the door, claiming I tried to escape."

"I'm a better man than that," Kokomo said, handing him his loaded gun. "Now git!"

Rick felt better the moment he stepped outside the jail and took a deep breath of fresh night air. It cleared his head and he wasted no time going around to the alley and coming into the Silver Dollar from the locked back door. Shoving the key into his pocket, he went upstairs and quickly packed his bags. He kept nearly a thousand dollars hidden away under a floorboard, and he took that and made a hasty exit out through the alley again.

He was weak from loss of blood and too much drinking, but he knew he could awaken the liveryman where he kept a horse and buggy, the same one that he'd used to take Jenny French on down to the Carson River where they'd become lovers so very long ago.

A half hour later he was on his way north to Reno. In the

morning, he'd sell his horse and buggy, then buy a train ticket for Denver. If he was lucky, he could pick up the pieces of his life and start over fresh.

Suddenly, he felt better than he had in years.

CHAPTER THIRTEEN

Ben did not arrive back in Virginia City until almost two o'clock in the morning, and he would have gone to Nettie Walker's place and slept the rest of the night, except that as he rode past the sheriff's office, he saw that the lamps were still burning.

Ben dismounted, tied his horse to the hitching rail and stepped inside to find Marshal Kelly pointing a gun at his belly. "What'd I do wrong now?" he asked. Kelly relaxed and put the gun away with a gruff, "I'm in no mood for fun and jokes. Sit down. We need to talk."

Ben took the only other chair in the office and straddled it so that his forearms were resting across its back. "What's wrong?"

"Rick Kilbane was in a shoot-out this evening. He killed two men."

Ben stiffened. "Self-defense?"

"Isn't it always with the Kilbanes?"

"What'd you do?"

"I tried to get him to draw on me so I could kill him," the marshal said matter-of-factly. "But he was too smart for that. I told him to get off the Comstock."

Ben sat up straight. Maybe he and Rick were on the outs, but that didn't mean that he would tolerate anyone trying to kill his old friend. "Why the hell did you want to do that if it was self-defense!"

"Because," Kokomo said, "I know that, if I don't kill him, sooner or later, you'll try and arrest him and he'll kill you."

"Now wait just a minute!"

"No, *you* wait," the marshal shot back. "Rick is a killer and you're not. He's also your better with a gun."

Ben came to his feet. "Maybe he is and maybe not, but that doesn't give you the right to bully him off the Comstock."

"I gave him a choice," Kokomo said. "He finally made the right decision. It's done. He left hours ago."

Ben shoved his hands deep into his pockets and strode to the door, then leaned against the jam. "I never thought he'd run out on his father. I thought he'd stay here to the end."

"I saved your life," the marshal said. "Now, I want you to help save mine."

Ben twisted around. "What's that supposed to mean?"

"It means that Ulysses is going to come after me and he hasn't much patience. You see, I branded him and Rick cowards and then I slapped Rick a couple of times in the face. He was drunk, but not quite so drunk that he didn't realize I'd have killed him if he'd reached for his gun."

Ben stood up and began to pace the floor in anger. "Dammit, Kokomo, you had no right to do that!"

"I had every right," the marshal snapped. "Maybe it wasn't by the book, but it was the right thing to do. Besides, I don't like waiting games. And this thing between the law and the Kilbanes was a waiting game. I decided to make the first move."

Ben thought back to the time he'd cleaned spittoons for

the Silver Dollar Saloon. He'd been a drunk then, the shell of a person, still trying to recover from the fact that he'd been the root cause of his father's destruction. Ben could recall in great detail the times that Ulysses had lost his temper and beat some poor devil half to death. He also remembered the times Ulysses had killed men in a drunken fit over a card game.

"Ulysses won't wait a single day," he told the marshal. "He'll come gunning for you in the morning."

"I don't think so," Kokomo said, exhaling a twin stream of blue smoke from his nostrils. "The way I hear it, he's been drinking too hard. He'll be shaky in the morning and he's smart enough to realize he needs to steady up before he braces me. He'll try something tomorrow afternoon or tomorrow night. Most likely, he'll bring help and I don't rule out an ambush."

"So you need an extra pair of eyes in the back of your head, is that it?"

"Exactly. But it means putting your life on the line."

"That's what I get paid to do," Ben said after a moment's consideration. He went over to a cabinet and took a couple of extra blankets out, then spread them on the floor. "But until the shooting starts, I better get a few hours of sleep. It's been a hell of a long day."

"It sure has. Let's just hope we survive to enjoy a lot more."

Ben stretched out on the floor and closed his eyes just as soon as Kokomo locked the front door and blew out the lantern. That accomplished, the marshal rocked back in his swivel chair, lifted his feet to the top of the desk and finished his cigarette in the dark. His chair protested as he ground the butt under his heel. Then he tipped his Stetson forward over his eyes to ward off a morning sun and went to sleep.

Ben listened to the man snore for almost an hour before he also drifted off to sleep thinking about Rick and how humiliated he must have been to be slapped in the face. Rick had always been prideful of his handsome face.

The prisoners woke them up early, and after they were fed their thin porridge and had complained all over again about the terrible food, Kokomo told them to shut the hell up or he'd step inside their cell and give them a real reason to gripe. The prisoners fell silent.

"So what happens now?" Ben asked.

"We go about our normal business," the marshal said. "Come on, I'll take you out to breakfast. I expect it will be noon before old Ulysses wakes up and learns that his son has flown the coop."

They had a good breakfast and patrolled the streets, nodding and tipping their hats to the ladies, stopping to answer questions from some of the businessmen about last night's shootings.

Mr. Kimball, the city postmaster, was upset. "Marshal, the Silver Dollar is only three doors north of our post office, and frankly, there's been so much shooting there that decent people are starting to be afraid to come pick up their mail and packages. Now, you were hired to spot this sort of thing. When you gonna do it?"

"Oh," Kelly drawled, pulling out his watch and studying it for a moment. "I'd say within the next twelve, maybe fifteen hours."

Kimball blinked with surprise. "Huh?"

"Have a good day, sir!" the marshal said as they continued on, leaving the postmaster in a dither of confusion.

They covered every saloon, and to Ben's astonishment, the marshal even poked his head into the Silver Dollar for a minute. He waved at a startled bartender, then stepped back outside to continue on, whistling a cowboy tune.

"How come, if you're going to be in a shoot-out, you're so damned cheerful?"

Kokomo shrugged. "I don't know. Maybe it's because I've never feared death. Even when I was your age. I believe in God and heaven, don't you?"

"Sure. But I still prefer to hold the jury on 'em for another fifty years or so."

The marshal chuckled. "You know, they say that the world was created hundreds of thousands of years ago. Maybe came from a star or something. Well, if you compare that much time against our own little lifetimes, you could say we don't live longer than the blink of an eye."

"*You* could say that. I could say eighty years or so is a whole lot longer than an eye blink," Ben argued.

"Well, the way I see it is that, when we die, we're dead."

Ben glanced sideways at the man. "You think we're going to be dead today?"

"I don't think so," Kokomo drawled, "but it would be a good idea to set our affairs straight."

"What affairs?"

"Well, you know. Who gets our stuff."

"I don't have much," Ben admitted. "Just some mining stock, that new horse I bought and the saddle."

"You got guns and a suitcase. You're wearing a watch and

chain and those are ten-dollar boots," the marshal said. "It all adds up to over a hundred dollars."

"I dunno," Ben said. "Last night when I rode up from Silver City, my horse went lame. If he's got a bad foot or something, he's only worth a couple of dollars."

"Ah," the marshal said, dismissing the problem with a wave of his hand. "I helped you pick that sorrel gelding out, didn't I? He's sound as a rock. He's probably just got a bruise on his frog and will be fine in a couple of days."

"If I don't get killed, I hope he's fine," Ben said. "I guess maybe I better leave a will though. I'm gonna leave everything to Mandy."

"I expected that," the marshal said. "But she doesn't need the horse, saddle and your gun. Just leave her the mining stock and your bank account. If you do that, I'll leave everything I got to you."

Ben stopped and looked at the marshal. "Why me?"

"Why not? There's nobody else."

"No sweethearts or kids or ex-wives or nothin'?"

"No kids," Kokomo grunted. "At least, not that I know about. As for women, I've had my flings, but none of them ever lasted once they found a man to marry who looked as if he might have a better chance of living out his natural span of years. Nope, I'm going to leave all I got to you. The only thing I'm asking in return is that, if you get killed and I don't, I get your horse, your . . ."

"All right!" Ben snapped, not wanting to think about dying any more. "You got 'em."

Mandy came into the office later that afternoon. She wasted no time with pleasantries but came right to the point.

"Ben, I heard about what happened last night. Rick is gone and Ulysses is raving mad, swearing he'll kill Marshal Kelly."

"Well," Kokomo said, "I hope he comes right at me. That'd make things a whole lot simpler all the way around. Either he'd kill me and I'd be done worrying about it, or I'd kill him and this town would be a whole lot safer for everyone."

Mandy took Ben's arm. "Are you in this too?"

"You know I am," he told her. "I wear this badge just like I'll wear a wedding ring, through the good times and the bad times. Thick or thin. Mandy, I can't run out now. I wouldn't have run out on your father and I won't run out on Kokomo."

"Tell him to run out on me," the marshal said. "Probably be the smartest thing to do. Go ahead, talk him into it."

But she stepped back and shook her head. "No," she said, "I know I'd be wasting my breath. And to be honest, I'm not sure that I'd be too proud of him if he ran away with me."

Ben grinned and hugged her. "That's my girl," he said. "That's the kind of woman that I fell in love with."

Mandy pulled away. She should have been pleased and flustered, but she wasn't. Her face was marred with worry. "I'm afraid for you both," she said. "I think Ulysses will do anything to kill you."

"We're expecting it," Ben said, drawing her aside. "The marshal and I are watching each other's backs every minute. We'll be all right. Now go home and stay away from me until this is finished."

"But why!"

"I just think it would be safer for you," Ben told her.

"He's right," Kokomo said. "If bullets start flying, you don't want to be anywhere close."

Before Mandy could form an argument, Ben gently prodded her out the door. "I'll be around soon," he promised. "And don't worry."

Mandy opened her mouth to say something, but then closed it and walked away.

"She's quite a young woman," Kokomo said. "You're a lucky man."

"That remains to be seen," Ben replied, standing beside the door and looking down the street toward the Silver Dollar Saloon, where a small crowd of men were gathered outside in anticipation of trouble. "Marshal, have you ever wondered how come folks like to see fistfights and shoot-outs?"

"Yep."

"What reason did you come up with?"

Kokomo scratched his belly. "They like to see other men's blood being spilled instead of their own. Makes 'em feel better."

"I don't understand that," Ben said.

"Neither do I. But that's the reason."

That evening when they prepared to go out and make their nightly rounds of the saloons and gaming parlors, Ben watched Kokomo Kelly select a sawed-off, double-barreled shotgun from the rifle case. The man had never carried a shotgun before and the vicious weapon's presence underscored the danger that they now faced.

"Maybe I should get one too," Ben said.

"Naw, but if I get shot, you might think about going for it. A shotgun like this can be a mighty good friend in a close fight."

Ben checked his own sixgun. He guessed he was as ready as

he was ever going to be. Both their wills were filled out and lying on the marshal's desk. It turned out that Kokomo had been squeezing his nickels and dimes by shaving the prisoners' meal allotments his entire career and was worth quite a bit of money.

"Let's go," the marshal said. "I can feel Ulysses waiting out there."

When they stepped outside their office, Ben's heart was beating so loudly that it sounded like a drum between his ears. He was scared, all right. Scared and almost wishing that he had taken Mandy and gone to farm in California. Mandy had pegged it right when she'd claimed this Comstock Lode wasn't worth his life. But then, there were some mighty fine people here and Ben reckoned that he was risking his hide for people—not for some great body of gold and silver hundreds and thousands of feet below Virginia City.

"We'll throw them off this time and reverse our normal rounds," the marshal said, shotgun resting across the crook of his left arm. "You just keep those young eyes and ears working overtime and we'll be fine."

They started walking, and when they came to the *Territorial Enterprise* office, Kokomo froze so suddenly that Ben, who had been a half step behind him, almost crashed into the marshal. "What's . . ."

He never had the chance to finish his question because, suddenly, gunfire split the night and it seemed to Ben to come from all directions. He jumped into the alley and struck a rain barrel, knocking it completely over and drenching himself as bullets swarmed at him like angry hornets.

Ben rolled deeper into the alley, hearing the probing shots biting into the wood, hitting the dirt and then ricocheting meanly down the alleyway. His gun was in his hand, but he could not see anything to shoot at. "Kelly!" he yelled, scrambling back toward the street on his stomach.

In answer, the shotgun roared twice and Ben heard men scream in pain. Then there was more gunfire and Ben saw Kokomo reloading. The man was behind a water trough and it was too dark to see if he was hit.

Ben returned fire and had the satisfaction of seeing the silhouette of a gunman pitch forward to lie still in front of the Crystal Bar.

"Nice shooting," Kokomo grunted. "Now cover me!"

The marshal jumped to his feet and Ben's gun was bucking in his hand as Kokomo tried to reach him in the alley. But the lawman had not taken three steps before a lone gunman stepped out in the street, took careful aim and fired.

It was Ulysses! Ben emptied his gun and saw the hateful old man stagger, then turn and disappear, heading for B Street just as Kokomo struck the sidewalk and rolled brokenly to a stop.

Ben was at the man's side, but there was enough lamplight to see a bullet hole dead-center in the spine, and when he gently rolled Kelly over, the town-tamer was struggling for breath. He reached out, hooked Ben around the neck and whispered, "Take . . . the shotgun! Kill him for me!"

Ben nodded. He pressed his face against Kelly's chest and heard the man's last lungful exit his body. In a fit of rage, Ben reached into Kelly's pockets and emptied them of shells. He picked up the shotgun and ducked back into the alley, reloading as he moved.

He hadn't known Ulysses all these years, not to be able to second-guess the man. Ulysses would go up B Street, but at the very first chance, he'd come swinging around and head for the back alley that led to his Silver Dollar Saloon. Like a wounded badger, Ulysses would take sanctuary in a familiar lair. In the Silver Dollar, he'd figure he had money, friends and protection. It was his fortress against any storm.

Well, Ben thought as he headed down the alley with the loaded shotgun clenched in his fists, this was one badger that was never going to reach its den.

Ten minutes later, Ben heard Ulysses coming. The old man was hit bad and his breathing was labored. Every footstep brought a grunt of pain from him, and when he finally reached the door, he fumbled into his pockets for his keys. That's when Ben stepped out with the shotgun.

"Good evening, Mr. Kilbane."

Ulysses was startled badly and his head snapped up to see Ben and the shotgun. He froze for a minute and then he relaxed. "Well, if it ain't the deputy. Hello, Ben! Come on inside and have a drink."

"Touch the door again and I'll pull both triggers," Ben said. "Just pull that gun out of your holster nice and easy, then drop it. This time, you're going to prison."

Ulysses shook his head. "You got it wrong, Deputy. I own the judge in this city. I'd get off scot-free and then I'd have to kill you for causing me so much trouble."

"I think you're right," Ben told him. "In fact, I *know* you are. You got off free the last time after you killed my friend, Sheriff Nye."

Ulysses straightened against the wall. " 'Course I did! And I'm glad you're seeing the way things are. Now come on in and have a drink. I can give you a job. Won't be cleaning spittoons, either! You and Rick were best friends once and I know he'd want me to treat you right, so . . ."

Ben let the shotgun slide down alongside his leg. It was cocked and pointing at his right foot. "Make your play, Mr. Kilbane. Just shut up and make your play."

Ulysses pushed out from the wall. "You're making a damn big mistake," he said. "I told you I'd treat you right."

"Make your play!"

Ulysses took a deep breath and went for his gun, but Ben was so powerful that he flipped the shotgun up one-handed and pulled the triggers. The shotgun belched smoke and fire, and Ulysses took both loads in the gut, almost tearing him apart.

Ben dropped the shotgun and walked away. He needed Mandy and he needed to think about farming in California.

CHAPTER FOURTEEN

Ben and Mandy were married two weeks later by the Reverend Morris B. Stroud at St. Paul's Episcopalian Church on the corner of F and Taylor Streets. The congregation sang "Rock of Ages" and the Reverend gave a powerful sermon on the sanctity of the marriage vows. Afterward, Ben and Mandy took the V & T Railroad down to Carson City where they stayed at the Ormsby House for three days before traveling on to Lake Tahoe where they extended their honeymoon to a full week. They would have liked to have gone around the lake and taken the Union Pacific Railroad from Truckee on over to San Francisco, but Ben decided that there just wasn't time.

"I'm the acting marshal now and I have a responsibility to uphold," he said one starlit evening as they walked a sandy beach near Emerald Bay. "I can't just be enjoying myself up here with you while things run wild on the Comstock."

Mandy had lived with a sheriff all her life. She remembered her own father saying much the same words year after year as his life passed. Her mother had tried to get him to take some time off, but he was duty-bound, and in the end, he'd died because of that duty. Mandy did not want to see the same thing happen to Ben. "But you hired a deputy before we left. Can't he take care of it just a little while longer?"

"No," Ben said. "He's green. Same as I was when I hired on. At least I had the benefit of your father's experience and then that of Marshal Kelly. This kid is a dead shot and he's quicker with a gun than I am, but he's inexperienced. A professional would chew him up and spit him out."

Mandy's hands twisted in her lap. "I hope the city council will find your replacement soon."

When Ben said nothing, Mandy added, "Do you?"

"I guess so." Ben smiled a little sadly. "I'll be honest with you, though. Being a lawman is sort of addictive. I'm not sure that farming is going to be nearly as exciting."

"There will be excitement enough trying to raise kids," Mandy promised. "And farming will be a lot safer. There is nothing to stop us from buying a farm now that we have the money."

Ben knew she was right. Marshal Kelly had left him enough money to buy at least a couple of hundred acres of prime farmland in California. Ben shook his head, remembering how surprised he'd been when the banker had told him of the amount of money that Kokomo Kelly had left to him. "I never even suspected until the day that Marshal Kelly died that he had more than two bits to his name. He was always trying to cut corners and make an extra few dollars here or there. I wish he'd lived long enough to have enjoyed his savings."

"Well, you're going to live plenty long enough," Mandy said. "But ever since you killed Ulysses Kilbane, I just keep thinking about . . . well, you know."

Ben sighed, "You keep remembering that nightmare and thinking that Rick will return to the Comstock seeking revenge against me. That's it, isn't it?"

Mandy nodded her head. "You know how he'd always do anything for his father. He worshipped that old viper and the man poisoned him until they were one and the same. Rick will come back when he hears his father has been shot to death, and he'll be wanting to settle the score with you."

Ben did not know what to say to that anymore. The subject of Rick and revenge had come up between them several times already and it always left them both feeling empty and depressed.

"Hey, listen," he said, linking her arm through his own. "We're on our honeymoon, in what must be one of the most beautiful places in the world. People are not supposed to be worrying about things on their honeymoon. They're supposed to believe there is no tomorrow."

Ben forced gaiety into his voice. "We're going to live to be old and wrinkled, with about a hundred grandchildren to bedevil us in our declining years," he said. "Tomorrow will take care of tomorrow. The only thing we have is today, and as for Rick Kilbane, my hope is that he's half as happy as I am, wherever he may be."

Mandy smiled. "Yes," she said. "Perhaps he's finally gotten some sense and married Miss French. That would be wonderful. But if we never see either of them again in our lives, you won't be too disappointed, will you?"

"No," Ben told her. "We were once best of friends, but we went in different directions. I think Rick always knew that we would, but I refused to believe it. At any rate, I don't expect to ever cross Rick's path again. Especially if he found Jenny French and is finally happy."

Rick Kilbane *was* happy, but restless and determined as he sat beside Jenny and sipped a cold glass of tea. Across from him sat Allan French, fifteen years older than his pretty sister, a respected editor and one of the most prominent men in Denver.

Allan was frowning at him as he said, "Rick, if you'll forget the damned Comstock Lode and take hold here in Denver, I can help you become as successful as anyone in the city. You've got all the tools. You're young, impressive in every respect and you know how to ingratiate yourself with important people. You can almost take your pick of the opportunities Denver has to offer and yet . . . yet you persist in this obsession of returning to the Comstock Lode. Frankly, I don't understand it."

Rick steepled his fingers and then he chose his words very carefully. "I don't expect you to, Mr. French. And there are some things that I can't talk about. Let's just say that I'm not someone who runs away like a thief in the night. I have a father. I left him without so much as a note of explanation."

"Then write him and explain!" Jenny cried, unable to control her frustration a moment longer. "Or send him a telegraph."

"That's not good enough." Rick set his tea down forcefully. "I have to go back and face him like a man."

"Do that and Marshal Kelly will shoot you on sight," Jenny said. "You told me that was his warning."

"I think he was bluffing. I think that if I go straight up to him and Ben, the marshal will realize that I pose no threat to either of them and that all I want is to see my father and explain why it's over for me on the Comstock. It's a free country, Jenny! I won't be banned from a place."

"It's pride," she said, trying to hide the bitterness. "What you really are saying is that you're too proud to just swallow being run off and let it go, even though you know Marshal

Kelly did you the biggest favor anyone has ever done in your life."

"He had his own reasons," Rick said, "and my best interests had nothing to do with it. I've got to go and set things right with my father. I have just decided to leave on the next train to Reno. With luck, I'll be back inside two weeks and then we can talk again, Mr. French."

Jenny stood up. She was angry but determined. "If you go, I'm going with you, and I'm staying by your side every minute."

"Jenny," her brother said, "I don't think that would be very wise." Jenny stomped her foot down on the floor. "Wise or not, I'm going!"

Rick looked at Allan and shrugged his shoulders. "I've learned what you've probably known for years—once Jenny sets her mind to something, it's as good as done. So I guess she's coming with me."

They arrived on the Comstock a week later. Rick was very quiet when they disembarked from the stagecoach and he took their valises, glanced toward the sheriff's office and then escorted Jenny toward the Silver Dollar Saloon. Rick was wearing his gun but hoped to avoid a shoot-out with Marshal Kelly. It was Kelly's choice, a man had to do what he had to do.

The moment Rick entered the Silver Dollar Saloon, he knew that some drastic change had occurred during his absence. Every head turned to him and the barroom fell silent. No one roared a greeting as they should have. In fact, no one said a damn thing.

Rick dropped the valises beside the door and pulled away

from Jenny French. "What's wrong?" he asked, moving toward the staircase.

"Mr. Kilbane?" the bartender said. "I think you'd better let me pour you a stiff drink."

Rick stopped in mid stride and turned to face the man. "Where's my father?"

"I thought sure you'd have heard by now," the bartender said, pouring both himself and Rick a full glass.

"Heard what!"

The bartender tossed his own drink down. "I can't lie to you, Rick. The fact is, your old friend Deputy Ben Pope caught your father in the alley and almost blew him in half with a sawed-off shotgun."

Placing both hands on the bar, Rick whispered, "When?"

"Right after you left."

"And where was Marshal Kelly?"

"Kelly is dead too. Your pa shot him just before he was killed. Way I hear tell it though, Ulysses tried to give himself up, but Deputy Pope just laughed and fed him both barrels of that shotgun. Didn't give him any chance at all."

Rick felt his insides go hard. "Where is Ben?"

"He was gone for a while. He's back now. I saw him heading for the post office out at the south end of town."

The bartender leaned forward. "I don't know if it matters, but Ben married Miss Nye last month."

"No," Rick choked, "it doesn't matter one damned bit!"

Another man stepped up and he reeked of whiskey. "Mr. Kilbane, this saloon belongs to you now, but it ain't the same without Ulysses. What happened to him in the alley . . . well, I saw him afterward and it was awful. There was blood and . . ."

Rick grabbed the man by the throat and slammed him over backward so that his head crashed against the top of the bar. The man's eyes filled with terror, but Rick let him go and he scrambled away.

Jenny French took Rick's arm. "Ulysses is dead! There's a train leaving soon, let's go and never come back here."

"No," Rick said, clenching his fists and smashing them both down on the bar. Picking up his glass of whiskey, he poured it down his throat and said, "This saloon is mine! *I belong here.* Ben has got to pay!"

Rick pulled out his gun. He knew it was loaded, but he wanted to check anyway, and when he was satisfied, he shoved the weapon back into his holster and started for the door with Jenny right behind him.

"Rick! This is crazy! You can't do this!"

But Rick guessed he could—and damn sure would—kill Ben Pope. Ben had always hated Ulysses for making him clean spittoons. He'd also hated him for killing his old friend Sheriff Nye—the man who'd have been his father-in-law and had actually been far closer than his real father. No, Rick thought, it's easy to see that Ben would have gunned Ulysses down without giving him any chance at all.

And now it was time for settling the score.

When Rick left, the saloon emptied in his wake. Even the bartender tore off his apron and raced out the door, leaving Jenny French alone. She could hear the sounds of men shouting and she was sure the entire population of this accursed town would be rushing to see two men shoot each other to death.

Time ceased to exist for Jenny as she looked around her, and it seemed as if the curse of Ulysses Kilbane was in everything she beheld. She could *feel* the man's evil presence! Trancelike, she walked up the familiar stairs, and when she reached the upper landing, she saw that the rooms were empty. The girls who had worked as she had once worked were gone. Ulysses' room was locked, but she knew what it would look like—every square inch of it, floor to ceiling. She shook her head as if she could erase the memory of what had happened to her in Ulysses' room during the first few weeks after her arrival on the Comstock.

Only one room failed to bring heartache and that was the one that she and Rick had shared together. But when she opened the door, she saw that Ulysses had flown into a rage when he'd learned that his son had fled Virginia City and he'd destroyed the room with maniacal efficiency.

Jenny clenched her fists at her side. This entire saloon was cursed and it was destroying Rick as surely as it had destroyed his father. Jenny marched across the room and found a kerosene lamp, one of the few things that had not been smashed to pieces. She knew where matches were to be found. She poured the kerosene across the rug, then struck a match and tossed it on the dark, spreading stain.

The flames leaped upward with a whooshing sound and immediately devoured the lace curtains she had once lovingly sewn. Jenny backed out into the hallway before she began to hurry from room to room making her fires. By the time she returned to the stairs, her face was covered with soot and her face was damp with perspiration. There was low roar as fire began to explode out through the open doorways.

Jenny walked slowly downstairs, hearing the inferno roar. She went behind the bar and found the best whiskey in the house. She poured herself another drink and raised her glass to toast a portrait of Ulysses Kilbane that captured his strength, but also his evilness. "Good-bye and good riddance," she said, drawing her arm back and hurling her glass at the framed portrait.

The glass shattered wetly across Ulysses' face and Jenny collected both her own as well as Rick's valise. By this time she could already feel the heat of the raging fire as it consumed the second floor. Outside she saw a huge throng of men about two blocks to the south and knew they were so absorbed in watching two ex-blood brothers kill each other that they would not realize their town was in danger of burning down once more.

To hell with them all, she thought as she marched down Taylor Street. She did not stop walking until she reached the V & T train depot, and then she stepped up to the ticket counter and said, "Two tickets for Carson City."

The kindly old ticket man smiled. "I don't see your friend, ma'am. Train is leaving in just fifteen minutes."

"If he's going to come at all, he'll be here by then," she explained, feeling her eyes begin to sting.

The ticket man's smile slipped. "Ma'am, maybe you better wait and see if . . ."

"Two tickets," Jenny said in a harsh voice before adding softly, "If you please."

"Yes, ma'am. Going far?"

She paid and received her tickets. "A long ways."

The old man started to say something else, but then he heard the St. Mary's steeple bell begin to toll a fire alarm. Fire had devastated the Comstock almost from its beginning, and on the dry windy mountainside, it was a calamity that drove terror into everyone's heart.

"You better get on board!" the old ticket man shouted, hobbling outside to stare at the plume of billowing smoke and flames that sprouted from the Silver Dollar Saloon. "Holy Cow! It's right in the middle of town!"

"I know," Jenny said without looking up at the mountainside. Hands clenched together so hard the knuckles were white, she took a bench seat and waited to see if her Rick would appear.

At the first toll of the steeple bell, the men of the Comstock had whirled, leaving Rick and Ben behind as they ran to help fight the fire that was already threatening to become a holocaust. Ben could see the flames, but Rick's back was to them.

"It's your saloon that's on fire," Ben called. "The Silver Dollar is going up in flames."

"Draw first," Rick shouted. "It's your only chance."

"Against you?" Ben kept moving closer. "I don't have any chance at all. Go ahead, make your play."

Rick's hand shook as he struggled within himself. "Why!" he screamed like a wounded animal.

"Ulysses was a killer. He was like a rabid dog. He wanted me to kill him so that you'd come back and kill me."

Rick's mouth twisted. "So that's the way you see it."

"He was no damned good."

"Neither was your father," Rick said, stopping at arm's length. "Forcing you to go down inside a mine. Thinking only of how big and proud he'd be when you worked yourself into an early grave."

Ben swallowed noisily. "I guess none of us are perfect."

Rick stared at him for so long that Ben thought he was in a

trance, and then Rick seemed to quiver and whispered, "Give me your gun and your badge."

"What . . ."

"Give them to me!" he raged.

It took Ben about one second to make the decision to unpin his badge and then unbuckle his gun belt and hand them to his old blood brother. "What are you going to do?"

Rick didn't answer. Instead, he looked deep into Ben's eyes, then pivoted around and started back up C Street toward the raging inferno that was leaping from building to building as Virginia City's volunteer fire companies rushed to contain it before it destroyed the entire Comstock. Ben followed Rick as close as he dared to the roaring wall of flames that had once been the Silver Dollar Saloon. He heard Rick shout something unintelligible and then saw him hurl the badge and gun belt into the searing conflagration.

Rick's clothes began to smoke. Ben grabbed Rick and dragged him back from the inferno.

"Water!" Ben cried.

Someone sloshed a bucket of water across Rick's smoking clothes and Ben shouted, "Dammit, Rick, what the hell were you trying to do—become a human torch!"

Rick's face was red and already starting to blister. His hair was badly singed and yet, he smiled. "Ben, it's done. All of it is finally done."

"Yeah," Ben said, relaxing because he knew his blood brother had not snapped and gone crazy. "So what are you going to do now?"

"I'm going to marry Jenny and take her back to Denver," Rick said, climbing unsteadily to his feet. He studied Ben intently, then added, "I threw away your damn badge and gun. They were going to get you killed, and probably sooner than later."

"I'm going farming."

Rick squeezed Ben's neck affectionately, and then he turned without another word and disappeared into the thick, boiling smoke to find Jenny French.

Ben's eyes were leaking tears and it wasn't all because of the smoke as he wondered how other men handled saying a final good-bye to someone they loved.

He'd think about that later. Right now, he guessed he'd better join a bucket brigade and help whip the fire before there was nothing on the Comstock to leave behind.

GARY McCARTHY is the author of the Darby Buckingham novels published in the Double D Western line, along with many other Western and historical novels. His most recent Double D Western is *Sodbuster*. He lives in Ojai, California.